LUNDON'S BRIDGE

AND THE THREE KEYS

MW01717213

LUNDON'S
BRIDGE

Dennis H. Christen
PARALIGHT PUBLISHING

Copyright © 2011 by Dennis H. Christen and Craig S. Zukowski

All rights reserved

PUBLISHED BY PARALIGHT PUBLISHING
a series of Paralight Films, LLC. PARALIGHT PUBLISHING, PARALIGHT FILMS, and associated logos are trademarks of Paralight Films, LLC

No part of this publication may be reproduced, stored in a retrieval system, or transmitted in any form or by any means, electronic, mechanical, photocopying, recording, or otherwise, without written permission of the publisher. For information regarding permission write to Paralight Publishing, Attention: Permissions Department, 5751 Buckingham Parkway, Culver City, CA 90230

ISBN 978-097181516-2

Second Edition, August 2011

This novel is based on a screenplay by Dennis H. Christen and Craig S. Zukowski
Proofreading and Copyediting by Paula Call
Book design by Sandman Studios (www.sandmanstudios.com)
Cover photograph of Paris Jackson by Charles Bush
Cover art by Sean Sullivan and Christian Perry, © 2011 Paralight Publishing

www.lundons.com

In Loving Memory of My Daughter

LUNDON SUZANNE CHRISTEN

November 9, 1976—March 26, 2008

You were with me from the very first word
and now you've gone and strapped on your wings.
I love you my Angel and know you are
watching over this project!
It all belongs to God!

It is said that nine out of every ten living things live in the ocean!

LUNDON'S BRIDGE AND THE THREE KEYS

Chapter 1

Prelude

The reason for the war was never really understood, especially by the children. If they had understood, the end may have been immediate. The most unfortunate thing about this particular war, the one between the fish kingdom and the humans; was everyone knew it had started because of the black mucky wall of sludge known by the fish-kingdom as the Decayed Sea, but no one understood how or why the humans had let it happen. It was a simple reason but one that seemed so complex that no one thought it was fixable, at least until the children began to understand it.

Many humans looked at the fiasco in the Gulf of Mexico during that terrible oil drilling accident that a British oil company had experienced in the early part of 2010. They acted as if that was the only thing that had ever happened to the ocean by the hands of the human race. But in reality, the fish-kingdom had watched the continued polluting of their world from many different human sources for a few hundred years, not to mention all the industrial muck deposited into the ocean during the entire last century.

Humans are funny that way; they like to blame the whole mess on the last guy with his hands dirty, but the fish-world wasn't so blind—they held the entire human race accountable. Every fish in the water knew the Decayed Sea had actually started to form many years ago. At first there were small sections of pollution around coastal areas where masses of humans lived, and the only thing that could survive inside the deadly muck was a type of sea-plant that while in clean saltwater was dormant and very tame—nonthreatening to anyone or anything, but once the plants were introduced to the polluted part of this sludge, they actually thrived on all the toxins and chemicals that humans had discarded into the ocean. By the time their bodies were sufficiently saturated with the poisonous muck, they had turned into meat eating predators and became a danger to anything that swam into their paths, and they didn't just wait for sweet tasting pieces of meat to float or swim by; they aggressively hunted their prey.

The larger and slimier the plants grew, the more they were able to free themselves from the planted state they'd grown up in and like the humans kicking their legs free from blankets while getting out of bed in the morning, were able to uproot themselves from the seafloor and use their long, stringy extensions as tentacles, propelling themselves forward allowing them to be more effective hunters. They would settle back down into the mud whenever they stopped for any length of time in order to digest their food or sleep.

Knowing that the whole of his ocean was slowly being polluted on a daily bases, His Majesty, King Pom, the Jellyfish king of the sea, had commissioned his top scientist, Jumper the Dolphin, to work hand-in-hand with his human counterpart to come up with something that would reverse the effects of the muck. With all the hoop-la that surrounded the oil drilling accident in that region which just happened to be where the royal palace was located, the king wanted to inspect the affected areas. He brought his teenage daughter, Her Royal Highness, Princess Pompom along with him to see everything for herself. His Majesty had hoped she would begin to learn why her mother, the queen, and he had put so much trust in the fish-world working successfully with the humans to fix this out-of-control problem.

Jumper and Princess Pompom were very close and had been ever since she could remember. He had been telling her for some time of his adventures with the human scientist and the exciting Muck Muncher experiments they'd developed. He had told her about the human scientist's young daughter, Lundon and that she would soon be able to meet the girl face-to-face. Princess Pompom was very much looking forward to that day.

According to the many reports His Majesty had received, the areas were growing at an alarming rate and it had started to be feared by all fish in the sea that not too far in the distant future, if something wasn't done about the problem from all over the world's oceans, the Decayed Sea could engulf the bulk of the earth's seas, seriously reducing livable space for the already overpopulated fish-kingdom.

As His Majesty's royal caravan approached the edge of the decayed section, suddenly and from out of the pitch-black dead part of the ocean, a high-pitched roar of a mutant plant monster broke the peaceful silence as it crashed through the black wall screaming its desperate want of something to eat. Its oil drenched mouth with long protruding teeth opened wide as it entered out into the fresh ocean water trying to reach one of the several soldier-fish that had dared to venture too close. With lightening speed the would-be victim darted back away, like a fly evading the thrashing flip of a fly swatter.

"Wow, that was too close to me tailfin, mahn!" squealed Hank, a hammerhead shark from off the coast of Jamaica. He turned to face his partner who was known throughout the whole of seven seas as Tenoch. He was a 450 year-old Aztec Warrior that had magically been turned into a giant squid by Paco, the magician of the royal court. He and Hank were two of the king's most trusted bodyguards and were always the forward scouts for the royal caravan.

"It's so unwise for him not to retreat! He's just standing there!" Tenoch said, staring at the daring mutant plant monster.

"It is acting as it be dying," Hank said, as he watched its every move.

"If the monster missed its prey during the first attempt," preached Tenoch, more like a professor than a military fish, "it could either retreat back into its safe haven, hungry; or it could take a chance on turning back into a non-violent state. The longer it is out inhaling clean ocean water, it is, in essence, purging its body from the mucky, poison elements that had caused its mutation in the first place. It only takes a matter of minutes."

"He's not going to make it, is he?" Hank matter-of-factly responded.

"Don't be so sure," Tenoch slowly said. "They thrive on the poison and to them, returning back into a passive sea plant is the same as dying."

The monster was fading quickly and within just moments, it began to change and before it could blink twice, its eyes started to bulge and soon its whole head looked like it was about to explode. Its leaves and stems all began to swell to twice their size as all the poison locked inside was being pushed out of every opening; forced out by the fresh, clean water now entering its system with each and every breath it took. Finally, the monster weakly and feebly fell to the ocean floor and with every ounce of strength it could muster, began dragging its withering leafed stems back into the dreariness of the polluted, dead sectors of its world—a world that it could breathe life-giving poison back into its system. After a few moments it was out of sight.

Twenty or so fin-lengths back from the wall of the decayed section, a cadre of soldier-fish from the royal caravan approached the location where Hank Hammerhead and Tenoch were waiting. This magnificent show of royal flamboyance of more than fifty soldier-fish surrounding several humongous stingrays—flat-ports as they are called by the inhabitance of the sea—carrying the jellyfish king, his daughter the princess, and their royal entourage would have fit the bill of a festival parade in any township up on land.

As jellyfish go, the Pom family was the most radiant species of jellyfish in the ocean; their bright pink, very transparent skin reflected a beauty that only sunlit water could reflect so brilliantly. Their body was larger than any other jellyfish in the ocean and was very regal and majestic in appearance.

The large flat-ports glided gracefully through the water like several synchronized swimmers performing an aqua-ballet. Small crabs, inside the opened mouths of the stingrays, steered the agile floaters by pulling on their long, elastic tongues with their claws, much like reins guiding a team of horses pulling a stagecoach.

Slowly the caravan pulled to a slow hover just a few fin-lengths away from the wall blocking them from getting any closer, and as the entire caravan came to a stop, Varkor, one of the scariest looking of any of the fish with the royal inspection team, moved up to the face of the wall as though he was invincible from any of its dangers. He was the captain of the royal guard, the highest rank in the king's service. His teeth were long and curved, sharp as a needlepoint and his eyes glared meanness and contempt for anyone that might try to float or swim into his path. He was armed to the gills with long, lethal spear-like quills that he could launch with deadly accuracy when needed.

Without warning another monster plant screeched through the mucky barrier grabbing one of the soldier-fish that was swimming next to Captain Varkor, swallowing it whole in one crunch of the plant's slimy, sharp-toothed mouth. A second later it was gone, but from inside the dark veil of slime, the sound of the mutant loudly chewing its meal could be heard by all the fish in the caravan.

"Your Royal Highness, fear not," Varkor smugly responded in a deep authoritative tone of voice as he noticed the king and his daughter approach from the caravan, "You and Her Majesty, Princess Pompom, are in no danger. It is, however, important that the truth be clearly known of how deadly this human made death trap has become. If not stopped, it will cover the whole of our world."

A handful of soldier-fish floating in the area between the royals and the wall moved aside in a reverent manner allowing the king to swim close enough to see how thick and mucky the water inside that section of sea had actually become. Before the king could get close enough to touch the wall, another mutant broke through the barrier heading right for the royal father and daughter. Before the king or the princess could make a sound, they were both grabbed from what must have seemed like every direction; pushing and pulling them into the darkness of the Decayed Sea where their world instantly turned deafly still.

The royal castle was more than thirty-reefs away from that decayed section of the sea; the fish method of measuring mileage in their kingdom. One reef was almost a mile in human measurements—give or take a few hundred yards. In the queen's bedroom located under the deep waters of the Gulf of Mexico, sat the greatest queen the kingdom of the sea had ever known. Like the king and princess, the queen was one of the largest of the jellyfish clan and radiated the purest of pink shades. Even the lighter shades let the light beams shine through from any direction and was the highest-grade of pink only the royal jellyfish family enjoyed.

Her Royal Majesty, the Queen, was stunningly beautiful in all respects and as always, gave Captain Varkor her total attention when he came to report. She had no idea, though; that this time the news he bore would change the course of her life from that very moment on.

Captain Varkor spoke in a whisper which only the queen herself could hear. The expression on her face clearly translated the words that the villainous reporter of bad news spoke. It didn't take long before her pleasant, happy expression turned to sadness, and as the words continued, her heart was haunted by what she envisioned and her mind grew darker still. Her eyes once crisp with clarity were clouded by visions of hate and revenge.

All the queen knew was that she had lost both her husband and her only daughter. She knew she did not bear this loss by herself, that all citizens of her kingdom shared the same sense of sadness and harbored the same desires of revenge towards their once human friends whom had shared the coastlines in peace throughout all the generations up to that time.

Whispered murmurs and distressing suggestions surged in every direction and carried across the whole of her kingdom. In the gracefully sculpted streets of brightened colors and beautiful corals, there was a great talk of war. Varkor's news of human engineered death and destruction of the sea's world tormented the queen to the point of no return, and finally she saw no other way but to enact her full and exacting act of justice.

LUNDON'S BRIDGE
AND THE THREE KEYS

Chapter 2

The Fish Kingdom's War Against Humans

Steam rose off the hot sand, except around the surf where the water cooled the air, and the surf thrashed up and back several times a minute, hundreds of times an hour, and several thousand times a day—every day of every year.

It was almost springtime and was a surprisingly warm morning, even for a Florida beach, as the tallest of the rare white-capped waves suddenly took on a spooky, translucent pink shade; and shortly thereafter turned into the form of the jellyfish queen of the ocean. Her body engulfed the whole of the large rolling wave as she opened her angry eyes methodically studying the vastness of the land. Then a gigantic oval mouth appeared; and as the queen spoke, her voice shrieked, reaching across the moist ground that stretched from the water's edge up to each of the weather-beaten homes that lined the small, sleepy oceanfront community.

"Humans!" bellowed the queen of the sea, "We all knew that every time my waters caressed your shores, it was a handshake, a promise of harmony between our two worlds. Why, then, have you broken that bond . . . killing my family—my child and my husband, the king? Had you not created the pollution that has destroyed more and more of my kingdom, countless numbers of my subjects would still be with us—with their families! For what you've caused I must take from your families as you have taken from mine. Beware, for I will soon be among you!"

As quickly as the giant jellyfish had appeared, it was gone, and with the breaking of the long, winding surf, the morning sun fluttered its sparkling golden beams over the western horizon like a flock of golden eagles flying high above the seaboard far below.

In one of the small homes that had long rested on a small parcel of seashore in picturesque Clearwater, Florida, 13-year-old Lundon O'Malley rose to the new morning. As she did every morning when she awoke, Lundon hurried to the foot of her bed where a humongous aquarium stood between the bed and the door to her bedroom. The tank was full of many different kinds of fish and the interior was nicely decorated with sand, seashells and all kinds of plant life. Whatever was inside that tank, though, you could bet it had come from the sea and not a pet shop.

Lundon and her mother had fixed her bedroom up with a collection of toys from Lundon's younger days covering the dresser, the small desk, and even the part of her bed she didn't use while she slept. Though she seldom played with the older toys, she didn't throw any of them away. To her they were trusted friends who always spent the night with her, keeping her company, like a big security blanket that made her feel warm and safe.

As bedrooms go, it was a nice, comfortable room for a cute early-teen girl, who, as she got older, was spending less and less time there, with more time spent at school, around the beach, in the water, or, of course, on the boardwalk.

One thing was for sure: If ever there was a kid born to live by the ocean, it was Lundon O'Malley. She could never imagine anything but a life where the grains of sand surrounded her toes more often than any pair of shoes or stockings ever did. The sound of the surf and the hungry flock of seagulls greeted her each and every morning, and bade her farewell at night.

When she was younger, she actually thought the seagulls squawking as they flew by, was their way of simply saying hello or good-bye in bird talk. It wasn't until she was five-years-old or so that she realized they were not actually talking directly to her. One day she even told her mother she didn't want to grow up anymore if she was going to start realizing sad things like that.

Lundon peered into the large aquarium at the base of her bed and carefully watched the movement of each of the fish until she spotted a little shark. It was the smallest fish in her tank, only about five inches long and looked weak and sickly but still able to swim. It had a large chunk of its dorsal fin missing from a mutant plant attack that happened the very day he was born. Also, one of its teeth was a real weird shape and hung out over its lip like a fang, and was obviously the reason Lundon gave him the name she did.

"Fang," Lundon cooed as her big round eyes lit up, "you can swim again!"

Through the flickering water of the aquarium, the blurred image of the bedroom door opening caused Lundon to smile. As usual it was her father, Kevin O'Malley, a fifty-something Irish American coming in to say good morning to his only child. Kevin was tall with a heavy-set, muscular build. His golden-brown hair was short and nicely styled. He looked more like a middle-aged surfer than a scientist.

"Look, Pops! Fang's gettin' better! You were right," Lundon reported.

"See, I told you it would work," Kevin declared as he bent down to take a closer look. "Now if we could only eliminate all the poison muck in the ocean."

"You can do it, Pops," Lundon proudly declared. "You are the smartest scientist in the whole world. You can kick muck butt!"

"Kick muck *what?*" Kevin asked with a big smile that spread across his face as he reached down for a morning hug. "Don't let your mother hear you talk like that! Anyway, it's not just being smart. Jumper and I both believe in what we're doing. You can do anything you want if you believe in yourself and believe in what you're doing."

"I believe in what *you're* doing," Lundon said with a cheerful optimism coming from deep down inside her. "How old do I have to be to start helping?" she asked in a part-demanding, part-begging manner that, at least when it came to her father, usually helped get her whatever she wanted.

"Well, it could be a really big job, and you know Jumper…he doesn't like quitters! If you start, you have to finish—no matter how tough it gets."

"Don't worry," Lundon declared without hesitation. "I'll never quit!"

"Are you sure?" Kevin asked, as he looked deep into her happy eyes.

"Well, sure, I'm sure," Lundon answered.

"Okay," he said, laughing. "Jumper and I need all the help we can get!"

They both knew what was going to happen next as Kevin and Lundon, both in perfect unison raised their pinky-fingers and interlocked them with both thumbs touching, symbolizing a sacred father-daughter promise—something they always did after making a pact with one another. It was something they'd been doing together ever since Lundon was four or five-years-old.

"Yeah, a pinky-promise!" Lundon yelled out.

"No it's not! It's a thumb-smoocher!" Kevin teased.

"A pinky-promise!" Lundon giggled back.

"A thumb-smoocher!"

"Pinky-promise!" Lundon continued to stand her ground, as she smiled from ear to ear.

"Thumb-smoocher!" Kevin said, as he laughed along with his daughter.

"Sparkles stopped by the boat yesterday and told me Jumper's comin' up today. Remember, Jumper promised he'd help you with your new flippers the next time he was here," Kevin added, reminding Lundon that it was going to be another fun-filled day in and on the water.

"Yeah! And Jumper promised to tell me more stories about Paco and Tenoch and Hank Hammerhead," Lundon added, letting Kevin know that she needed absolutely no reminding of the plans for when Jumper joined them again.

"Oh yes, Tenoch," Kevin fondly added. "He was an Aztec Warrior who, because he became so tired of all the violence and killing on land, wanted to join the world of the sea, and so Paco, the royal magician of the ocean, turned Tenoch into a giant squid. You know, by now that old squid has lived in the ocean for over four hundred years protecting the fish kingdom from all the many enemies that have come and gone over the centuries. It's a great story…and it's all true! I've actually met them all."

"Wow!" Lundon squealed. "Mom should hear this. Maybe she'll come with us this time, and then I can show her how good I swim," Lundon said, as she ran out of her room, heading toward the kitchen, feeling that for sure she had just the right ploy that would make her mother want to join them on the boat that day—what with Tenoch and her mother both being Hispanic and all.

Kevin, on the other hand, did not think Lundon had a prayer of getting her mother to join them out on the water that day, and his expression showed it. He knew Sonia didn't think filling her child's head with too much 'fantasy' was all that good of a thing. She believed that children today have way too much 'make believe' in their lives and would rather see more educational oriented thoughts filling Lundon's head. That was a major issue she had with Kevin and his approach to sharing his job with their daughter. Especially now that Lundon had become a teenager. Nah, Kevin knew their boat trip wasn't going to be a part of Sonia's day, no matter how much Lundon begged.

In the small but well-kept kitchen, Sonia was ironing Lundon's pretty Sunday-go-to-meetin' dress for church. Breakfast was already prepared and sitting on the table and stove. Like Lundon's room, everything was laid out in perfect order—spacewise. The colors were bright and clean and everything matched, including the many Mayan knickknack figurines placed on shelves and countertops everywhere. Even the toaster had a landscape of some Mexican village painted on its sides.

Between the aroma of a freshly cooked Sunday breakfast and the smell of slightly damp cloth being smoothed out with a hot iron, one could instantly see that the O'Malleys' place was a true "home sweet home."

Sonia, a very beautiful, dark-haired woman in her mid-forties, was already dressed in a stunning go-to-church outfit. She was a descendant of the Mayan civilization and was born and raised in Cancun, Mexico. Sonia had come from a very close-knit family. Sonia's father and grandfather were college professors; Sonia had been a high school English teacher and even after marriage and immigrating to the U.S., had never given up the desire to teach. Outside of raising a family, teaching was her life's dream and her English proficiency was impeccable, with only a slight accent on a few sounds. After arriving in the United States, she attended school part-time trying to earn her teaching certificate so she could someday become a schoolteacher in her adopted country.

It was the 'schoolmarm' in her that made Sonia want to teach Lundon everything and she enjoyed sharing with Lundon the fun of reading books. It was partially because Sonia had spent endless hours reading to Lundon from an early age that Lundon possessed the imagination she did. As far as Sonia was concerned, though, that was good and bad. But when it came to Lundon's and Kevin's love of the ocean, well, Sonia wished that it did not play such an important role in their lives; and if the truth were known, she was a little jealous of it.

"Mom?" Lundon yelled as she rushed into the kitchen, not taking the time to notice the smell of fried bacon and scrambled eggs. "Do you wanna watch me swim with Jumper today? He's gonna tell us a story about a Hispanic squid—a giant one!"

"Lundon, honey!" Sonia responded with a warm smile on her face. "Aren't you forgetting something?" she asked as she reached down and softly wiped some of the sleep from Lundon's eyes.

Lundon reached up and gave her mother a big kiss and hug, assuming that was what she had forgotten. "Good morning, Mother!" Lundon said, thinking only about trying to convince her to join them out on the boat. Then with all the hope she could muster in her best adult-like voice, she asked, "Well? Do ya?"

Sonia and Lundon had gone over that very request so many times that it was getting harder and harder for Sonia to justify the reason why she would not—could not—go with them out on that boat.

Luckily, before Sonia had to answer Lundon's anxious question, Kevin walked into the kitchen and took his place at the head of the breakfast table. He knew he had made a big mistake making plans to go out on the boat on yet another Sunday, and Sonia's cutting stares thrown his way let him know she was not happy about it.

"Please, Mom," Lundon continued to beg as she took her seat.

"Lundon!" Sonia sighed as she moved to the stove to get the rest of the breakfast.

"But Jumper's comin' up!" Lundon begged, trying her best to circumvent the answer she knew was about to come rolling out of her mother's mouth.

"We can be back for the afternoon service," Kevin added, hoping to give Sonia a way to allow them to go on the boat and still feel that part of her cherished family's day at church would be saved.

"Is that a promise, O'Malley?" Sonia asked, refusing to continue until Kevin agreed by nodding his head. "I guess I can use the morning to study for my teaching certificate."

"Why don't you come with us?" Kevin asked, surprised at himself for even asking.

"Oh, *please*, Mom?" Lundon begged. "Don't ya wanna see me swim?"

"Lundon! Mommy would love to see you swim, but you know how frightened I am of the ocean."

"But Jumper can help you not be afraid," Lundon said, trying one last time to convince her mom.

Sonia looked toward Kevin, her eyes pleading for some help—any help.

"Mom can see you swim another time," Kevin answered, trying to keep Sonia from having to suffer any further. "Hustle now, we don't have much time."

There was no more talk during that rushed meal. Sonia knew in her heart that she was missing something very special and important to both Lundon and Kevin even though, as far as she was concerned, most of it bordered on make-believe. She bit into a crunchy piece of bacon as she continued to justify her feelings. For some reason, fear of the water was much more powerful than even her desire to participate with the two people she loved the most.

LUNDON'S BRIDGE
AND THE THREE KEYS

Chapter 3

Time Ran Out

Sea Wonders Research One was the name Kevin's boss tagged onto the big research boat. If Kevin had his way, he would have called it *Lundon One* or just plain *Lundon*. The sleek vessel belonged to Sea Wonders, Inc., a marine research company that Kevin had worked at for more than 10 years. Kevin had full access to the large boat. His department was a one-man show; well a one-human show because there was his dolphin partner. But talking only human, he was the only player on the stage, which suited him just fine.

His boss worked on the opposite coast of Florida and that, too, pleased him. Not having to go to 'the office' each and every day meant he could be free to arrange his hours so as best to coordinate Lundon's school time with his work schedule. He had the freedom to be with Lundon as much as he could. Sometimes he would purposely not go on the water until Lundon came home from school so she could join him and share in the overall excitement of his work. Something she did with 100 percent gusto.

'Old Blue,' what Kevin and Lundon called the boat, was large, and the science lab onboard was state-of-the-art. Kevin and his dolphin buddy, Jumper, a scientist of high distinction, worked tirelessly to save the ocean from continued destruction by the ever-growing Decayed Sea. The Decayed Sea was not actually the reason Kevin was hired at Sea Wonders, Inc., but it had seemed to dominate 90 percent of his and Jumper's time over the last several years. Even with the extra burden caused by the 2010 drilling accident by a British petroleum company, they were doing everything they knew and more to try and solve the muck problem in the ocean.

Many of the beaches in that part of Florida were narrow sections of landmass that paralleled the coastline and you couldn't get to them without the several bridges that connected the small islands to the mainland. At the ends of each island, there were more bridges connecting the strips of land to each other. The water between the land and the beach islands made a perfect harbor for almost any size of non-commercial vessel. There were small rowboats and large yachts, motor boats and massive sailboats all parked in boat slips. For a boat to get out of the harbor area, it would have to head for the closest break of one beach-strip to the next and float under the large bridge connecting the two.

The large slip where Kevin kept Old Blue was more than a mile away from the entrance to the open sea. The time it took to get out of the harbor drove Lundon crazy because she liked the faster speeds where the water could spray up into her face. In the harbor area the boats could only travel…well, let's just say with her fins on, Lundon felt she could swim faster than Kevin drove the boat.

Lundon always knew when they cleared the entrance because Kevin would turn the boat north and gun the powerful engines, causing the wind to almost whistle and the waves to splash with each up and down bounce the boat took. Kevin always took the same route parallel to the coast. They were never more than 200 yards away from the beach and from where Lundon sat; she could always look east and see the coast. She knew every section by heart, and knew that when she could spot Clearwater beach and her own house, they were getting close to where Kevin would stop so he could rendezvous with Jumper for work.

As expected, that Sunday afternoon turned out to be warm, bright and sunny, perfect for a fun-filled day out on the water. As the boat finally sped up, Lundon, sitting in her safety chair her daddy had built just for her, was wearing her life vest and holding onto the side of the boat so she could get the most out of the rushing wind and the spray of the waves. With her new flippers at her side, she smiled as she counted the beats out loud from one to four, closing her eyes each time she finished saying the number three. She knew the fourth wave would shower her with its fresh, salty spray.

"One, two, three, spray! One, two, three, spray!"

"One, two, three, spray!" she screamed out again as she closed her eyes seconds before the cool water splashed onto her face.

Still, the time couldn't pass by fast enough for her whenever she was expecting Jumper to come up. Even with her frolicking in the salty mist of the sea, each second seemed like a minute and each minute felt like an hour.

Stored in a bin on the side of the boat near where Lundon was cooling herself with every fourth wave was Kevin's surfboard.

Hand-etched on the top portion of the board was the name and inscription: *Kevin O'Malley, the Irish Dolphin.* The letters had been burned into the surface of the board with a wood-burning knife and then lacquered over several times to keep it totally waterproof. It was very obvious, by the look of the surfboard, that Kevin was a serious surfer.

"Look at Waxer cut those curls!" Kevin yelled from the captain's deck, pointing across the water toward the direction where the 18-year-old boy was skillfully gliding over, under and through, the medium sized waves. From the look of his ability on that board, it was obvious he'd soon be ready for the larger waves found much farther south. It was never really talked about, but both he and Kevin knew what was just around the corner for Waxer. He dreamed of being a world-class surfer.

Waxer's real name was Warner W. Worthington, but for as long as Lundon could remember; the only names he would allow anyone to call him were either 'Waxer,' or 'The Great White of Florida.' He fancied himself as having the look, the walk, and the cool of a shark. Lundon couldn't remember ever seeing Waxer without one of his three shark tank-top shirts.

The very first day Waxer met Jumper, some two years before, Jumper gave him the 'Great White' nickname and Waxer was really proud of it. He wore it on his shirt like a war hero sporting medals. Though he identified with a shark over any other fish in the ocean, his real reason for liking the nickname was that Kevin had been the only other person Jumper had given a moniker to. He felt honored to be considered in Kevin's league, especially by Jumper.

Kevin had taken Waxer under his wing when Waxer was only a toddler. Kevin knew that Waxer didn't have a father and, not having a son himself, found it to be a sweet, natural blend of friendship. However, Waxer never thought of Kevin as a father. In his own mind, it was more like having a big brother, a teacher, or a kindred partner of the sea.

Waxer probably would not have admitted it to anyone, but he considered Lundon a sister, and even though they argued a lot, Lundon loved him like a brother. She couldn't remember not knowing him; he'd always been around.

Kevin and Lundon waved their arms high into the air, letting Waxer know they were paying attention to his surfing savvy. He was so good at it he could wave to someone and not miss a beat, no matter how fast the curl was moving. Moments later, Kevin pulled the big boat to a stop and, as he released the anchor, Waxer paddled up to them, handed his long surfboard to Kevin and climbed up into the boat.

"You're really crazy on those waves," declared Kevin. "I'm impressed!"

"You were right. I just needed to move closer to the tip," Waxer reported, smiling about the kudos his teacher was throwing his way.

"You've learned all you can on that old long-board," Kevin said as he moved toward his own, much shorter surfboard. "I want you to have this."

"You mean it?" Waxer asked in a somewhat subdued voice, as though he didn't think it could be true—like Kevin was just teasing him.

"Yep! It's a lot different..." said Kevin, still with a teacher's warning in his voice. "With this smaller board, you'll be able to feel every move the ocean makes—you'll become a part of it.

Then, and only then, will the ocean's powers become yours and you'll be ready for the bigger waves."

Realizing that Kevin wasn't joking about giving him the surfboard, Waxer allowed himself to believe the thing was actually his. He was so happy he could not take his eyes off it. He held the board up and carefully ran his fingers over Kevin's name burned on the face. It had now been handed down to him and he couldn't have been more thrilled, even if he had been given an Olympic gold medal.

"This is so sick! Thanks Bro," Waxer said, still not taking his eyes off his new gift.

Kevin, knowing exactly how his young friend felt, smiled at Waxer's obvious love and respect for his old surfboard, then turned and moved toward the laboratory. "Let me know when Jumper pops up," Kevin said as he disappeared inside, shutting the door behind him.

Wanting to be ready for when Jumper arrived, Lundon reached for her new fins. After she put them on, and without missing a beat, she looked up at Waxer, recalling the argument they had apparently not settled the last time they were out on the boat.

"Okay, Waxer! Remember, you said you didn't believe me about the magical swamp? Well, if you still don't believe me, you just ask Jumper when he gets here."

"I already told ya," Waxer snapped, reminded of the unpleasant conversation and quickly showing that he did not want to get back into the same old word-war with her. "If it was true, Jumper would have told me a long time ago. He's never mentioned a magical swamp so I know you're just making it up!"

"I did not just make it up! Ask my dad, then," said Lundon,

angry at even the mention that Jumper hadn't really told her the story. "Maybe Jumper thought you were too old to care about a magical swamp anyway! I don't know why he didn't tell you, but he really did tell me! Maybe he likes me better than he likes you!"

"Yeah, right!" Waxer said as he turned away from Lundon and reached down inside a large metal bucket and pulled out a bar of surfboard wax. He didn't want to spend another moment of his time talking about Lundon's fairytales. He knew that if Jumper had a story about a magical swamp, he for sure would have told him about it before he would have told her. Besides, nothing was going to take his mind off his new prize. He started rubbing the wax over the smooth surface, and it wasn't long before he was so into his own fantasy of surfing large mountains of slick, glassy ocean waves that even if Lundon had continued on with her never-ending conversation about her supposedly made up stories, he wouldn't have heard one word of it.

Kevin had all but finished getting into his neoprene diving suit as he moved over to a large worktable. The cabin, though smaller in size than a professional lab, housed a full-blown science lab. Well, full-blown as much as what Kevin and Jumper needed, anyway. It was full of all kinds of computers and fish tanks—more tanks than anything else. They were literally everywhere, and housed a variety of sea plants as well as several other unrecognizable 'things' from the ocean's floor. Each exhibit had a handwritten label attached to it indicating what was going on inside. Each label had data explaining the progress of whatever was being tested, with dates, times and phase progress notes.

Kevin moved to the largest aquarium in the center of the lab. It took up the entire middle section of the lab. Above it was a white card with the number 209 scribbled on it and below that was a photo of what was being tested, or at least what it looked like six months before pollution had changed it into something totally unrecognizable. The once-vivacious and brightly colored sea plants had turned dark brown, stringy and lifeless, and the formerly clean seawater was dirt-black and grit-oily. It would have been considered by some as pure, undiluted poison.

Of course, it was reprehensible to Kevin, who was a member of the species that bore the brunt of the blame for the pollution in the sea. As a representative of that offending population, he took it as a personal challenge to do everything in his power to try and find a solution to the problem.

"Day 1 - 8 - 0," Kevin said as he turned on his small hand-held tape recorder, making sure he did not miss even one syllable as he spoke succinctly into the microphone. "Six months have passed since I started introducing poison samples from the Decayed Sea into Exhibit 209."

He then took a chunk of tuna fish from an opened can, smelled it, and after he was able to catch his breath again, dropped the rotting piece of tuna down into the dingy water in the tank.

"First attempt to see if there is still any life left in plants," he continued as he watched for any response to the bait. The speed with which things started happening surprised him. "Holy...!" spat Kevin as he moved closer to the glass, not believing his eyes.

The slimy, lifeless plants inside began to move, growing more and more violent as they lunged for the meat, snarling and fighting each other for a taste. The ocean's native plants had evolved into ugly, despicable, mutant, meat-eating sea monsters. Pulling their roots out of the mud, they swam all around the large tank, sifting for even a small morsel of tuna.

Kevin wondered what the plants growing in the Decayed Sea must look like after all this time. They must be gigantic, he thought, and if they were anything like those in his lab, he knew that the whole fish kingdom was in serious trouble.

Kevin quickly moved to a clean exhibit, reached inside the muddy bottom and took a handful of his and Jumper's own creations. They called them Muck Munchers because they were designed and bred to devour the deadly man-made poisons of the polluted water—restoring life-giving nutrients back into the aquatic environment. And, of course, both Jumper and Kevin fervently believed the Muck Munchers would be the very weapon that would destroy the Decayed Sea.

The Muck Munchers spun from a hypothesis Kevin had created, but it took Jumper's firsthand knowledge of sea-life genetics to make their creation possible.

The creatures were cute in a scary-looking kind of way, and were a cross between a crab, without its shell, and a catfish with three heads, one growing out of the plump body, and two growing from the drooping jaws of the main head. Each head had two oval eyes and a large oval shaped mouth, and the smaller two heads had crab-like claws growing out of their long, extended necks. The main head had blue-green eyes and a much larger mouth. It could, unlike those of the smaller heads, suck in muck from the ocean with great force. The smaller mouths were designed for nothing but eating the mutant plants or any other potential threat that would or could be dangerous to its purpose. They used their claws to grab and hold the mutant plant as it happily devoured each morsel, mouthful-by-mouthful until there was nothing left in their claws. On the surface, it was starting to look like it might be the most successful experiment of Kevin's and Jumper's partnership.

Though the Muck Munchers were fierce fighters when it came to the mutant plants, they were gentle creatures to humans. They loved to be cuddled and kissed and they enjoyed kissing back. They had been created to live off unwanted, polluted or rotted debris man had discarded into the sea. They were like living filters—ingesting dirty water in through the mouth and squirting clean water out the other end—the butt-end.

Kevin moved back to tank number 209 and dropped the handful of baby Muck Munchers into the water.

"Wow! Look at those little Muck Munchers...," Kevin said but quickly stopped, thinking he sounded unscientific. He cleared his throat and continued watching, a little shocked at how naturally aggressive the Muck Munchers sucked when put into dirty, polluted water, and likewise how mean and fearless the mutant plant monsters were as they attempted to eat the Muck Munchers. As the Muck Munchers opened their mouths wide and sucked the dirty water into their bodies, they would immediately spray out clean, nutritious water through their backend, all the while trying to keep the plant monsters from taking a bite out of them. From the suck-in to the let-out, it only took a matter of a few seconds.

Kevin began to smile. It looked like their hard work was really starting to pay off, and as he continued observing, one of the baby monster plants successfully caught up to a smaller Muck Muncher and as the three-headed youngster opened wide and inhaled a mouth full of mucky water, the mutant bit down hard on the muncher's backside, but before it could rip and tear, the little Muck Muncher yelped out of three mouths at the exact same time and then pooped a burst of clean water into its attacker's mouth.

Within seconds the plant fell to the tank floor and as several other Muck Munchers rushed to that location in the tank, they too turned their butts toward the struggling plant and let their loads squirt, straight into the breathing stream of the monster and within seconds, all the black, muck rushed out of every pore of the small sea plant and was sucked out of the water by the larger heads of the several munchers swimming above the dying mutant plant. After a moment more of weak resistance, the monster turned back into the beautiful sea plant it once had been.

Again, trying to sound as professional as he could while he lifted his arms high in the air, Kevin continued. "Observation: Within moments, Muck Munch...I mean, creatures...literally extract the toxins out of the water and mutant plants subsequently choke to death in clean water."

Kevin could not hold back as he clapped his hands and smiled a big, 'we finally got it' smile. Then, trying to appear more like a scientist he continued recording his thoughts as he observed the results of his now-successful experiment.

"I must continue to monitor for the exact number of creatures required to terminate mutation versus the amount of water volume. Time: 10:36 a.m., Sunday."

Though Kevin had expected the mutant plants to react violently, he was ecstatic to see that their Muck Muncher experiment had worked, at least in the first phase of restoring the mutants back into a dormant, non-aggressive plant form.

Kevin began to pace back and forth, again throwing his arms high into the air and twirling around in circles. The more he thought of the possibilities, the more energized and animated he became. It was very obvious that Kevin had difficulty acting like a sophisticated scientist. Even Sonia teased him about it not being in his DNA.

"It's Jumper!" Lundon yelled from out on the deck. "Jumper's comin'!"

"Yes!" Kevin answered. He finally had some real results to show Jumper. He grabbed his dive mask and rushed out to the main deck.

Lundon was standing up, pointing at a dolphin that was swimming straight for them. There were several other dolphins in the water behind the one that was headed their way.

"Can you see him? He's comin'!" Lundon said as Kevin stepped next to her. "Where did he go?"

Right in front of Lundon's face, Jumper popped up from under the water. Of all the dolphins Lundon had ever known, and she had known many, Jumper was the cutest and the smartest. His face had a wide mouth with teeth that glistened brightly in the sunlight. Unlike other dolphins, though, Jumper had salt and pepper colored eyebrows and a wavy lock of hair protruding from the top of his black-gray forehead. To Lundon, Jumper seemed almost human, and to add to the mystique, he could speak several languages, English being one of them.

That day, however, Jumper's expression was somber and forlorn, and he was winded and out of breath, as if he had just swum a 100-mile marathon to get there.

"You're not going to believe how successful our Muck Muncher experiment has turned out! I'm telling ya, those little suckers...," Kevin boasted, but stopped cold as he looked into the eyes of his finned partner. "Jumper? What is it? What's happened?"

"It's King Pom and Princess Pompom," Jumper said pausing for a breath or two. "They've been killed, eaten by the mutant plants!"

"What? No! How?" Kevin asked, realizing that some of his worst fears had come true.

"They were with Captain Varkor and several of his soldiers inspecting the expansion of the Decayed Sea," Jumper said, as he stared up into the eyes of his friend. "Kevin! Varkor has convinced the queen it was you humans that created the mutant plants in the first place. She has declared war against the entire human race."

"We humans have made a mess of things!" Kevin declared. "But we've got to show her our Muck Munchers can clean it all up! I just saw what they can do!"

"Really? They worked? Wow! I'll take enough with me now to show Her Majesty—if she'll even listen. It might be too late. Word is that she's fixated on revenge, and war is all the entire kingdom is talking about now," Jumper said, glancing over towards Waxer and Lundon as though he'd just realized they were there listening. "We must get more to the palace by tonight. Can you do that?"

"The little critters were hatching at a pretty good rate the last time I was down there. Take a couple of pouches now and I'll get some help and be ready for your dolphin-run later tonight. Make sure the dolphins show up right after nightfall," Kevin said as he slipped on his air tanks and flippers. He then pulled his dive mask down over his eyes as he looked at Waxer. "Watch things up here, Waxer! I'll be right back up after I've supplied Jumper with a couple of pouches full of Muck Munchers. It's show-n-tell time!"

With that, Kevin looked at Lundon. It was obvious that she was sad, but she seemed to be okay. He slipped down into the water and he and Jumper were soon out of sight.

Lundon couldn't take her eyes off the water; the sadness on her face showed that the news about Pompom, the young jellyfish princess, had broken her heart. Jumper had told her that it wouldn't be too much longer before the two would be able to meet face-to-face. She believed Princess Pompom, though older, would have been the kind of friend that would have been forever. Tears began to fill Lundon's eyes and trickled down her wind-dried cheeks.

LUNDON'S BRIDGE AND THE THREE KEYS

Chapter 4

Lundon's Belief is Tested

Kevin understood that getting home late and missing church was going to be hard to explain to his wife, especially after having made the big 'we can be home on time' promise that very morning. He hoped Sonia would understand...you know, without having to explain anything. But he guessed the chance of that was less than one in, oh, say, ten trillion. He wished he could explain what had happened to poor King Pom and his sweet, innocent daughter, Princess Pompom, but he knew Sonia would not be able to wrap her head around the fact they were even real, let alone that they had been killed, too.

"Oh, Momma!" Lundon said, with tears still in her sad, and by now, red-streaked, eyes. "Princess Pompom is dead! She and her daddy got eaten by plant monsters."

Wanting to stop Lundon from saying another word, Sonia raised her hand and placed it gently up to Lundon's lips. Sonia had finally had enough. "I don't want to hear anymore make-believe coming from you. You are too old for such nonsense!

Especially any that makes you feel so sad. Now go and get washed up for dinner."

"But, Momma!"

"Lundon!"

"But . . . ?"

Sonia gave Lundon that 'I mean business' look and Lundon reluctantly moved toward the bathroom. She could not understand her mother's lack of remorse over the unfortunate demise of her special friends from under the sea. To Lundon, make-believe had absolutely nothing to do with the King and Princess. They were real and she knew it.

Still, Sonia had wanted to put her foot down about these imaginary characters in her daughter's life, but now that Lundon was crying real tears, she knew she had to put a stop to it once and for all. Make-believe was supposed to make you laugh and feel happy, not cry and feel miserable! Enough was now more than enough, as far as she was concerned, and she was going to finally do something about it.

Kevin moved to the phone, knowing by the manner in which Sonia had responded to Lundon that he was in for it—*big* time. Sonia didn't say anything at first. She just sat and watched him, her hands loosely clasped together and resting on her legs. By this time in their marriage she knew which buttons to push and that night was going to be the 'torture him with silence' button.

"Yeah, Rolley!" Kevin said as he tried to ignore the penetrating, x-ray-like stares coming from his wife as the voice on the other end of the phone answered. "I forgot to mention that I'm out of air. Can you bring some spare tanks with ya? Great! Yes, I'll explain everything to you at the boat. I'm on my way now."

Kevin figured that would be all he would have to say about anything; after all, telling Rolley while Sonia was listening was like telling both of them. All he had to do now was get his dive bag off the table and pray that she would give him a kiss and wish him Godspeed. Yeah right! Not in his lifetime.

Instead, Sonia continued to stare him down as he walked over to his dive bag and picked it up off the table. Missing church had been the last thing on his mind, but he also knew deep in his heart that he was not going to get anywhere without dealing with her at some point. He had to make her understand what he was working on out there in the ocean was not just a child's game. He needed to make Sonia understand that Jumper, though a dolphin, needed him to follow through with getting the Muck Munchers shipped out to him that night more than he'd ever needed Kevin before and that was all there was to it.

"It's an emergency!" is all Kevin could spit out of his mouth, and knowing that it was kind of a lame statement, one that he's used too many other times, he tried extra hard to give Sonia that sometimes-convincing 'I know what I'm doing' look. After that didn't seem to work either, he just said, "I *have* no choice! I have to dive tonight!"

"I was worried sick that something terrible had happened," Sonia said softly but with a slight undertone in her voice, and still sitting as she was when he and Lundon arrived home. "Forget breaking your promise about church. Why didn't you at least call me? Look what time it is! You know how much I worry when you guys are out on that ocean."

"Oh, honey..." Kevin said, trying to sound as convincing as possible. "I didn't mean to worry you. But, please try and understand..."

"No!" Sonia sputtered, putting her hand up in the air, interrupting him. "You've gone too far with this storytelling of yours. Kevin, look at your daughter! She's in tears for heaven's sake!"

"But you don't understand..." Kevin said, trying once more to explain.

"Oh, I understand all right. I know that you spend all your time hanging around with a dolphin that you claim can talk. You even told me that he was a scientist—a colleague. It's bad enough inventing stories about jellyfish kings, queens, and little princesses, but now you have plant monsters eating them, too? Honey! It all simply has to stop. I want you to tell Lundon that none of it is real! She's not a little girl anymore!"

"I can't tell her that!" Kevin said, staring at her for the longest time. "I know it sounds pretty weird, but it's all true. If you would only come out with us just once, then you can talk to Jumper yourself!"

Sonia was silent; she stood there searching her soul, facing something maybe for the first time in her life. By the look in her eyes, Kevin realized that after all this time; his wife, Lundon's mother, might actually be ready to join them on the boat. *Had he found the right words this time?* He thought to himself as his heart started to race. He placed his bag down on the floor and took her in his arms.

"What is it that you're really afraid of? Is it your fear of drowning or is it that you are afraid to let yourself believe in something that seems impossible?"

A different look appeared in her eyes, a look Kevin had never seen before.

"Maybe both!" Sonia slowly answered as her thoughts fluttered over what she was thinking about actually doing. "Could I talk to the dolphin too?" she asked double-checking his resolve.

Kevin simply smiled and nodded his head.

"And the dolphin will answer me back?"

Again, Kevin nodded.

"I think . . . I think for Lundon's sake, I'd better go and see what is really out there!"

Lundon, coming back into the room from washing her hands, had heard Sonia's last statement. Lundon ran to Sonia's side, wrapped her arms around her waist and said, "Oh we're gonna have so much fun."

"Okay, young lady," Sonia said with more resolve in her voice, "you and daddy are going to have to protect me."

"Jumper will help too," Lundon said, happier than she'd been for a long time.

Kevin reached down and pulled his daughter closer to the two of them for a group hug.

"Maybe I should have agreed to this a long time ago. Well, you don't want to keep Rolley waiting too long, do you?" Sonia whispered as Kevin slowly pulled away wondering what he was being set up for.

"I almost forgot about him!" Kevin smiled, as he kissed Lundon and then Sonia, then reached down and grabbed his dive bag off the floor. "Wait till you meet some of the fun little Muck Munchers, Sonia, you'll want one for a pet, right Lundon?"

"Yep, she sure will," Lundon responded, as she and her mother playfully pushed Kevin out the door. "Be careful Pops! I love you!"

"I love you too." Sonia added as Kevin walked away from the front of the house.

"It's a BIG double ditto!" said Kevin as he hurried off in the direction of his boat.

Pulling the boat up to set the anchor, Rolley and Kevin prepared for the night dive. Like the O'Malleys, Rolley lived close to the beach and loved his life around the water. Though he didn't scuba dive much anymore, he sometimes helped out when Kevin needed him.

"This'll be a dark one. Stay close!" Kevin warned.

"I do remember the dangers of a night dive, ol' buddy," Rolley said as a smirk came to his lips. "There is one thing I'm curious about, though."

"What's that?"

"Am I going to run into any talking fish?"

"And what would you do if you did?" Kevin joked.

"Ah, come on! You're kidding, right?" Rolley asked.

"Maybe..." Kevin answered, smiling as he slipped down into the water, pulling his dive bag with him. Rolley didn't know how to take that answer as he, too, disappeared under the darkness of the night surf.

Rolley, like most of the O'Malleys' friends who lived along the beachfront, teased Kevin about his and Lundon's unyielding claims of talking dolphins, royal sea creatures, and such. Though they didn't actually think that Kevin believed it, they, like Sonia, figured it was for Lundon's benefit, just a fun little game of make-believe to help make the time seem a little more exciting.

On the ocean floor, about 200 yards out from the beach, Kevin and Jumper's Muck Muncher spawning farm was about 40 feet below the surface and was nestled below a set of underwater cliffs. To give the spawning farm the look he wanted, Kevin had constructed a picket fence around the small area where the newly developed creatures were hatching from under the mud. The fence was held to the ocean floor by several heavy iron spikes that served as anchors. From a distance, it looked much like a strawberry patch, with furrows and rows of mud, all arranged in a straight line from one end to the other. The only difference was it was not a patch of land in some field in farmland, USA.

There were also rock sculptures of cows, horses and several huge statues of fish surrounding the spawning yard. Kevin had even put a stone leprechaun figurine at the entrance, hoping to spruce the area up and give it some personality—an Irish flare of humor.

Rolley smiled and shook his head in disbelief as he looked the place over. Kevin knew Rolley would get a kick out of how he'd taken the time to create a real farm look, even down at the bottom of the ocean.

The hatching process was in full swing as the newly birthed Muck Munchers, needing no help from anyone or anything, wormed their way from under the muddy furrows. The three-headed creatures crawled, heads first, while their bodies took more time surfacing from the waterlogged sand.

The hatching Muck Munchers resembled animated plants, sprouting from under the ground; their three heads moved in opposite directions like vines of a rose bush growing in fast forward. As each of the heads individually searched for food, their mouths opened so wide they could have consumed a softball whole, without any trouble at all.

When Kevin and Rolley reached the patch where the Muck Munchers were hatching, Kevin pulled out several pouches from inside his dive bag passing a handful of them to Rolley. Kevin began placing the Muck Munchers that had emerged from their earthen wombs into the pouches.

The funniest trait of each Muncher, though, was that each head spoke perfect English. Each one also had a different personality from his or her parent's head. Each one would be jabbering away at the same time, sometimes arguing with each other and sometimes just talking to other Munchers totally ignoring the heads from their own bodies. It was very comical and Kevin figured that Rolley would especially find it amusing.

Rolley, trying to follow Kevin's lead, squeamishly reached for a Muck Muncher but quickly pulled back as the closest creature jetted up to eye level with him. It looked at first as if it was going to smile and nod, but it instead it spoke, "Hey their gramps, what's new?" and then it bolted forward; locking onto Rolley's entire face like it wanted to French kiss him but didn't know how to.

"Bubble be me! You just had to do it, didn't you?" said one of the smaller heads of one Muck Muncher swimming up out of the sand to watch the antics of his fellow muncher.

"Hey back off there," screamed one of the smaller heads of the Muck Muncher that had latched onto Rolley's face. "Course he had to do it, what did you expect him to do, he has to do what he has to do, that's all!"

"Yeah," hollered the second head of the latched muncher, "you're just jealous!"

"Jealous is it?" mocked the first head of the three headed fish. "If it was me, I'd rather latch onto an oversized oil clump, but to each his own!"

"Ah! Leave 'em alone, will ya?" squealed the larger head of another Muck Muncher that had joined the excitement. "The human asked for it if you ask me!"

Rolley didn't know what had hit him. By now there were several Muck Munchers swimming around him talking up a storm, some for him and some against him. The affectionate Muck Muncher had latched on from the top of the forehead to under his chin, engulfing Rolley's dive mask and breathing apparatus. For a moment, Rolley felt as though his whole face would turn out to be one big hickey. Rolley pulled with all the strength he could muster but couldn't force the determined little love bug to let go. Its body was so elastic that it just stretched with the force of Rolley's pulling power. He took his finger and started tickling the rubbery creature in any place on its body he could. Finally, not being able to squirm away from Rolley's wiggling finger, it let go.

Rolley crammed the laughing Muncher into a pouch and then glanced over at Kevin, then down towards another Muncher as he pulled it from the sandy ocean floor. This time he kept it away from his face as he stuffed it into the same pouch with the French kissing Muck Muncher.

"What's a matter air boy? Afraid we might suck your brains out through yer nose?" hollered the large head of another one Rolley now held in his hand far away from his face. All three heads of that mouthy Muncher laughed and continued to taunt him until they were crammed inside the large pouch that Rolley was filling up.

Rolley had known for a while that Kevin was involved in some kind of research for Sea Wonders, Inc., what with his big lab boat always anchored in the same place and could be seen from the beach area. What he didn't know, however, was that Kevin and his dolphin partner, Jumper, had actually crossbred crabs and catfish to create the strange-looking aquatic mollusks he was cramming into those pouches. He couldn't believe they were really talking. That was one of the reason's he let the first critter get so close to his face, he couldn't believe words were actually coming out of its multiple mouths. He continued glancing towards Kevin but Kevin was busy filling bags with his own set of jabbering Munchers. He'd already filled four bags by the time Rolley was just going for the fourth creature. He did eventually begin to work faster, ignoring the barrage of comments coming from the mouths of his newfound buddies.

Once several of the pouches were full, Kevin motioned for Rolley to bring them over to him. On his way there, suddenly and from out of nowhere, several dolphins bolted into Rolley's light beam, startling him. Realizing they were not sharks, he looked at Kevin and motioned to inquire whether these were the famous talking dolphins, or not.

Kevin motioned that they were in fact talking dolphins, and then very nonchalantly proceeded to attach one of the pouches to the lead dolphin's nose. The dolphin nodded his head at Kevin and was off with lightning speed, headed for the fish kingdom deep in the ocean.

Kevin signaled for Rolley to do the same with his pouches, and as Rolley found himself face-to-face with a dolphin, he stared for a time not sure what to do, hoping this mammal wasn't going to lip-lock one on his face, too.

"Well, dummy, take the straps of the pouch and loop them over my nose," the dolphin finally said very slowly as he moved his nose about two inches from Rolley's face like a drill sergeant getting ready to yell a command at a slow thinking recruit. "And they say fish are slow to take the bait. Come on man, times a running out!"

Finally Rolley got it as he hurried and placed a pouch onto the dolphin's nose. The dolphin smiled like he had really enjoyed the one-sided conversation and then darted off to his dark and distant destination.

That was it; Rolley had finally heard it all with his own ears and was happy Kevin had finally trusted him enough to let him share this wonderful and very magical part of his life. Rolley didn't need any more orders barked at him and soon had all his pouches on their way to Jumper and hopefully the queen.

Kevin moved over closer to the base of the cliff wall that climbed high above the farm area where yet another group of Muck Munchers were ready to be gathered and transported. If it wasn't for that cliff dropping down the way it did, the water in that area wouldn't be more than 10 or 15 feet deep. As Kevin prepared to fill more bags, the remaining dolphins began darting anxiously back and forth in front of him like they were trying to prevent him, for some reason, from getting any closer to the cliff.

Heeding their warning, Kevin stopped swimming as large air bubbles shot out from inside the core of the wall. Rolley, too, stopped what he was doing and instinctively started moving toward Kevin's location to see what was going on.

Sensing something was not right, Kevin gestured for Rolley to stay back, and as he did, a small part of the wall started to crack—spreading quickly into the form of a large mouth. Opening wide, schools of pink colored bubbles, in the form of a large tentacle shot out and grabbed Kevin's arm with a powerful grip—a stinging grip.

Kevin tried to free himself, but the bubbles were too powerful and he couldn't pull himself free, then, without warning, another bubbled tentacle, then another, and they began pulling him deep inside the cliff's interior. It was like the whole cliff had come alive and was trying to swallow Kevin whole. Kevin struggled with all his might but knew he was going to lose that battle.

Rolley began swimming toward the cliff, ignoring Kevin's warning to stay back, but by the time he reached the location, the wall had closed with Kevin locked deep inside. Kevin's dive bag was the only thing remaining. One of its straps had been pulled into the opening, but the mouth had closed tight before swallowing the whole bag. It hung there suspended only by its strap. It was like the cliff had turned into a monster and with its mouth opened wide had swallowed Kevin whole.

Panicked, Rolley tried to pull the bag free from the cliff wall but it was now a permanent part of the rock with no signs at all that there had ever been an opening. After several attempts to try and get it free, Rolley realized he would need some help to try and rescue Kevin. He hated to leave Kevin alone there, but he understood full well there was no other choice. If he didn't get some help soon, Kevin wouldn't make it. At most, he figured another 20 minutes of air was left in Kevin's tank.

Rolley knew he could not swim up to the boat too fast because of the chance of getting the bends or what divers called, decompression sickness. That could end up killing him and then what good would he be to Kevin? No! He knew he had to get to the surface as fast as he could but within the limits of safety.

The remaining dolphins, sensing the danger too, looked at each other and then at Rolley as he floated upward. Within a few seconds they took off for the fish kingdom at jet speed.

The Beach Rescue Unit of the Pinellas County Sheriff's Department was on duty and in the water within a few short minutes of Rolley's call. They searched all night long and well into the morning of the next day, but with so little air left in his air tank, everyone knew that Kevin could not still be alive. Everyone, that is, except Lundon.

Sonia's eyes were swollen and red from the long night of crying. She sat on her living room sofa, tissues in hand, and stared out through the large picture window at the ocean. Lundon sat on the floor next to Sonia. She tried from time to time to console her mother, waiting for the chance to tell her it would all be okay. She couldn't understand what all the fuss was over. Lundon knew her daddy was only spending some extra time down there with Jumper. After all, she heard firsthand that they had to work hard to get the Muck Munchers to the queen in time. What with everyone coming and going—policemen, firemen, scuba divers, friends and rescue officials—all asking this and wanting to know that, Lundon couldn't get a word in edgewise.

Waxer was there, too. He stood leaning against the wall next to the front door, listening to all the hollow words coming out of people's mouths. The surfboard Kevin had given him was propped against the wall next to him. Waxer was more confused than he was sad. He knew the real story about what Kevin and

Jumper were up to, and he was waiting to hear firsthand what Rolley had to say about everything. Only seconds had passed since the last visitor had gone when Rolley entered the house carrying Kevin's dive bag in his hand with one of the straps missing.

"We couldn't find anything!" Rolley said as he broke the short-lived silence that filled the room. "Not a trace! Just his bag."

"Explain to me how a cliff wall could have swallowed up my husband?" Sonia softly asked, as her frustration continued to grow. She tried hard to comprehend what had happened to her husband—to her family, to her life, but no one had any answers for her.

"I can't explain it, Sonia! I'm trying to figure it all out myself. All those talk..." Rolley said, almost to himself before he stopped midsentence. "It's the strangest thing I ever saw," Rolley said as he turned to Waxer. "Waxer, I've seen you swimming with *that* dolphin many times. Come on dude; tell me, did it talk to you, too?"

"You were there with him. How could you let this happen?" Waxer asked. "If you haven't found Kevin yet, then he must be...," Waxer stopped and looked down toward Lundon. He didn't want to say what he was thinking, not in front of her. He looked back at Rolley. "He and *that* dolphin were the only friends I ever had." Waxer grabbed his surfboard and left the house not saying another word.

After a moment of reflection on what Waxer had said, Rolley turned back to Lundon. "Lundon, I really need some help here. Do you know how your daddy made it so those little three-headed creatures could...you know, ah, talk? I mean, he created them, right?"

"You mean the Muck Munchers?" Lundon asked. "Uh huh. Jumper and Pops made them. But they're not the only fish that talk, all the fish talk."

"Come on Rolley! You only think you heard them talk. Now you're sounding crazy. Weren't you down in the ocean—under the water with him—them?" Sonia said in a very defiant tone of voice.

"You might very well be right there!" Rolley answered, not paying much attention to Sonia's comment as he continued to look directly at Lundon.

"Is that what your daddy called them?"

"Yep! He'll tell you all you want to know when he comes home," Lundon declared without the slightest bit of doubt in her voice. "He might even show you some."

"Last night when I was helping your daddy, we gave several dolphins pouches full of those Mud Munchers," Rolley stated.

"No," she laughed, "it's M U C K Munchers, not Mud Munchers."

"Ok! All right, Muck Munchers. Do you have any idea where the dolphins were taking them?" He asked, hoping more than expecting to get a real answer.

"To the queen, silly! They had to show 'her Royalness' how well they could eat the muck out of the ocean. Then she wouldn't have to go to some war."

Rolley had surmised that the dolphins were being used to spread the creatures around to different parts of the ocean. Not in his wildest thoughts had he imagined they were being delivered to a fish queen somewhere.

"I'm sorry, but I just don't understand any of this," Rolley said as he looked down at the cut strap of the dive bag and then back at Sonia. "I'm going to find out what is happening out there...even if I have to go talk to *that*...I mean, to Jumper myself."

"Well, if you talk to Jumper, you can just ask my dad. I already told you they are together!" Lundon said, now realizing that she finally had the floor. She turned and faced her mother.

"Jumper's my friend!" Lundon said as she took her mother's hand. "Jumper and Pops will come home soon. Dad and me need you to believe that!"

Sonia could see that Lundon was trying hard in her own way to make things better. Sonia knew, though, it was supposed to be the other way around. She was supposed to be the one comforting the child, not the child comforting the adult. Sonia reached down and pulled her daughter up to her, hugging her tight.

"I love you little girl! I love you so much!" Sonia finally worked a smile to her lips. "By the way, young lady, it's 'Dad and I,' not Dad and me!"

"I love you too, momma. I really, really do!" Lundon echoed as she hugged her mother back, hoping her mother was hearing the message and not just the words. "Daddy and I need you to believe!"

Chapter 5

Sonia Refuses to Believe

Three months had passed since Kevin made that night dive with Rolley, and Lundon still had not wavered in her belief that he was going to come home when he and Jumper were finished with their work down in the fish kingdom. It was just taking longer than they had planned, that's all.

Even under the circumstances, Lundon remained a happy and contented child, whether she was home playing with the special fish friends in her tank or keeping busy with various projects that interested her. It could have been collecting things; making objects out of sand and seashells, or just having a story from one of her many books come to life right in front of her eyes. Spending time thinking of her father and what he was doing also played a large role in keeping her mind busy. She remembered the promise she'd made to him about never quitting and she knew that also meant never giving up in her belief in him.

To help pay the bills and continue going to school Sonia took a job as a manager of a new candy shop that had been built on the boardwalk. It was called the Taffy 'N Stuff, and sold a variety of candy and ice cream treats, and featured as its main attraction was saltwater taffy. Since most of Sonia's day was now spent at work, Lundon found a spot on the sand just down from the boardwalk where she could play but still be within sight and sound of her mother. That section of the beach unofficially became Lundon's piece of sand.

On one particular day, Lundon was sitting on the sand in her normal place just a few feet away from the surf when Waxer, carrying his surfboard, approached on his way to his new job. He was wearing his Taffy 'N Stuff t-shirt over his normal attire which, of course, was his "Great White of Florida" tank top and cut-offs. You could see the outline of the shark through the work t-shirt.

Waxer had always been teased about his tank top and people wondered if he ever took it off, even to shower. He was one of the first people Sonia hired to work with her at the shop. However, with his surfing schedule first on his priority list, even over a few mandatory summer school classes, the job turned out to be just part-part-time.

"What's up?" Waxer asked as he stopped to see what Lundon was doing.

"Nothin'!" Lundon said as she stared out over the vastness of the ocean. "I'm just thinking about Jumper and Pops."

"Really? It's been three months and Jumper hasn't come up to see us even once," Waxer somberly said. "Hey Lundon, do you think that Jumper only liked us because of your dad?"

"No!" Lundon said. Then after a moment of thought, continued, "I don't know."

"Haven't you ever wondered why he hasn't come back to see us?"

" 'Cause he's busy helping my dad!"

"That's what I would have thought too, if I was only, how old are you now?" Waxer asked.

"Thirteen! Don't you remember? You were at my birthday." Lundon answered.

"Yeah, Thirteen. But that's old enough to be able to huh, let the, let it, you know, go!" Waxer said, stumbling with the words.

"Let what go?" Lundon asked.

"Look Lun! What I'm tryin' to say is that your dad is, well he's dead and we have to let him go! Otherwise, you'll end up like all the whacked out customers my mother brings around the trailer who believe she can bridge the living with the dead. Dude! I'm telling ya, it's not true! You have to let it go," Waxer said as he turned toward the stairs, leaving Lundon totally confused about everything. She thought for a moment then called out to him.

"Waxer? If Pops were dead, Sparkles would've told me! He's not dead!"

Waxer stopped and turned around. "I've been out there every day waiting and watching. I haveta believe that Jumper doesn't care about us! You know what? Maybe he never did...Or maybe he's dead too!" Waxer turned and hurried up the long wooden stairs that led up to the boardwalk.

"They're not dead!" Lundon said, not really thinking about that though, she was stuck on what he'd said earlier. "Waxer? Wait! What about a bridge? Waxer? What did your mom say about a bridge?"

Bang! An idea popped into her head. Her eyes lit up when she realized Waxer had given her the answer she'd been looking for.

Almost ready to open for the day's business, Sonia was helping the other two girls do the last of the set-ups by the time Waxer reached the shop.

"Hello, Waxer. How are you this morning?" Sonia politely asked, looking up from the counter to greet him.

"Hangin' in there, I guess," Waxer said.

"You look tired," Sonia said, always acting like a second mother to the boy. "Did your mom have another late..."

"...night séance? Yeah!" Waxer said, interrupting her. "Can you believe she wants me to be like one of her wacko customers and bridge myself to Kevin in the...HEREAFTER."

The very mention of Kevin stopped Sonia in her tracks, but seeing the look on Waxer's face and the expression in his eyes as he verbalized his mother's words, she realized he was still obviously grieving the loss of his friend—his best friend. Sonia knew that Kevin and Waxer were close, but she was truly taken aback by what she was seeing in that young man's eyes. She had just assumed that after all this time he had pretty much learned to deal with the whole matter and had moved on with his life as she had tried to do.

"She says," Waxer continued, mimicking his mom's voice, "You'll find inner peace, and you should quit being such a hostile little boy."

"I'm sure she loves you very much. She's only trying to help you deal with your loss."

"Yeah, right! What ya got for me to do?" he asked, clearly wanting to talk about something other than his mother.

As Sonia pointed to several boxes she needed for him to throw away, Lundon approached from the beach area holding several Popsicle sticks in her hand. "Can I have some glue?"

"Glue? What for?"

"I'm gonna build a bridge outta Popsicle sticks," Lundon proudly declared.

"Okay! But stay where I can see you!" Sonia warned as she reached for the half-used bottle of glue and handed it to Lundon.

"Okay! But do you haveta say that in front of everyone? I'm not a little child you know!" Lundon answered as she took the glue bottle.

Right next to where she was standing was a 'free sample' bowl stuffed full of taffy. Attached to the bowl was a sign that read, 'Free Sample Take One!' Lundon reached up and took a handful but before she withdrew her hand, she slowly, one-by-one, dropped the taffy back into the bowl until she was holding just one. Smiling, she was off to start making her Popsicle-stick bridge.

As Sonia wiped down the counter, she noticed Waxer's surfboard that Kevin had given him. Waxer had burned his name in the board under Kevin's.

"He's kept the ol' tradition going..." Sonia whispered to herself. Her mind was filled with thoughts of Kevin. She remembered sitting on the sand, safe and dry as she watched him prove, time and time again, that he and his board, that board right smack in front of her, were one with the ocean—his ocean.

She missed Kevin and she was sure thoughts of him would dominate the rest of her day. They always did when something—even something small—reminded her of him. But still, she was happy to see that Waxer loved and cherished Kevin's surfboard as much as Kevin had. That meant a lot to her, and she felt it would have meant a lot to Kevin, too.

That very same night, down the beach on the other side of the tracks, so to speak, was Wanda Worthington's trailer. Wanda was Waxer's mother, and the two of them lived in the small mobile home. Well, Wanda lived in the trailer and the only nights Waxer would sleep inside was when it rained. Other than those nights, he slept out under the stars. That didn't bother him as much as not having a real place to bathe or a private place to change his clothes. It was an old trailer and only had one room. The kitchen, the bedroom and the dining room were all in the same space. Waxer's bed was built above the kitchen table and from the stove and fridge, you could shake hands with a person who was in bed, sitting at the table or standing at the front door.

What had been the bathroom, Wanda turned into a closet for their clothes. Both Wanda and Waxer used the public restrooms at the beach for their showering and use of the toilet. Waxer could not remember living any other way; but now as he was approaching adulthood, it was starting to bother him.

Wanda was a Korean-born psychic medium, a fortune teller, and was always working with people who needed her special talents. She'd met Waxer's father while he was in the Army stationed in Seoul, Korea. They married and when Waxer was 7 months old the Worthington family moved to the states.

Wanda quickly adapted to life in America and, like Sonia, learned the English language very quickly. Though she was much too young to have experienced the sixties, she felt she'd lived a previous life as an American hippie, and felt strongly about continuing her quest for life's answers—answers most of us did not even know there were questions for.

Waxer did not remember anything about Korea except he did speak Korean and usually spoke it when he spoke to his mother and although he was half Korean, he looked more like his father. Speaking of his father, he didn't remember anything about him either. Waxer hadn't even turned one year old by the time his father left the family, which was shortly after arriving in Florida from Korea.

As she did most evenings, Wanda had a customer that night, too. That was great for the family income, but it made Waxer crazy. He didn't have much room in the small trailer that he could call his own as it was, and when his mother had a client, he had to wait outside until the whole ceremonial thing was done. Like most young boys, when they arrived home from a day out of the house, they want to hit the refrigerator. It's just a thing kids do but because of customers, the fridge may as well have been on the moon.

Sometimes Waxer would sit for hours before Wanda had finally finished with her appointments. The older he got, the harder it was for him to understand why he had to live that way. He did not believe in the same things his mother did, that was for sure, and to add to it, he was becoming more and more angry about his life at home and with the feelings he was harboring about Kevin and Jumper abandoning him, he was at a breaking point.

Wanda's customer that night was a man by the name of Dwight Seletz. He was a normal kind of a guy, in his forties, and about three years earlier had lost his mother to old age. Dwight had been coming to Wanda's place for several months and was pretty confident that he would soon make contact with his mom.

He and Wanda sat across from each other. Their hands were clasped together with their arms resting on top of the small kitchen table as they looked upward, eyes tightly closed with optimism radiating from their faces.

"Emille Seletz!" Wanda summoned. "Answer! Dwight is here waiting for you to speak. Emille? If you hear me, speak to us..."

Waxer arrived home after his long day of surfing and working at the taffy shop. Tired and ready to call it a day, he stopped to set his surfboard on its rack next to the trailer. As he reached for the doorknob he hesitated, looked at the pair of men's shoes neatly placed on the welcome matt in front of the step leading into the trailer, then leaned closer to see if he could tell how far into the séance his mother was. The expression on his face turned sour. With Wanda just getting started imploring the spirits, he knew it was going to be another night of sitting outside waiting until who knows when, before he'd have any access at all to his precious little space inside.

"Emille Seletz! The bridge has been made, cross over it now."

Waxer pulled back away from the door with disdain running through his nerves.

"Yes! I can feel you! Emille! Come closer!" Wanda demanded.

"I can feel her, too!" Dwight said. "Mother! Mommy? I'm waiting."

"We are losing her," Wanda muttered. "It's like she don't know your name. Quick! Another name...a nickname. Did she have a nickname for you?"

"Doodoo Dingle!" Dwight yelled. "She called me Doodoo Dingle!"

Wanda's left eye opened a crack after hearing that name. She studied him over for a moment, and then closed it again, trying desperately to keep the powers flowing. She knew it didn't take much to break her concentration and she hoped hearing a dorky nickname like that wouldn't break the flow. It was all she could do to keep from laughing as it was.

Waxer laughed to himself, thinking that Doodoo Dingle was a perfect name for an obvious loser. But then, suddenly he thought of something he could do to entertain himself while he was kept waiting for the Doodoo Man to speak to his mommy. He turned and walked around to the other side of the trailer still laughing.

"Emille Seletz!" Wanda continued. "Emille Seletz! Doodoo is a here. Come! Unite with us from your loft on high."

After all these months of trying to contact his mother, to Dwight's great delight, a voice suddenly answered back. Since all other voices had channeled themselves through Wanda's voice, she was stunned as she sat there looking at Dwight, wondering to herself what was going on.

"Doodoo Dingle! Is that you?" cried the faint but high-pitched voice.

"Mommy! It's me, your little Doodoo Dingle. I'm here!" cried Dwight, overcome with emotion.

"Doodoo Dingle. You don't understand," responded the voice, as it grew louder.

"I don't?" Dwight questioned, confused at what he did not understand.

The voice was coming from down below, and instantly Wanda knew what was happening, but Dwight apparently had been expecting the voice to come from above for some reason.

"Mother? Why is your voice coming from down there?"

"Oh, Doodoo! You were always such an IDIOT," screamed

the voice. "I'm burning in hell, Doodoo Dingle." Outside at the rear of the trailer, just under where the kitchen table was positioned, Waxer was on his back with his head raised so that his mouth was close to the floorboards. Hardly able to contain his laughter, he continued screaming at the top of his voice, "Hurry! Run, Doodoo! The devil knows where you are! He's coming to get you! Run...Run, Doodoo Dingle, Run!"

Waxer then put his arms up and started shaking the floorboards of the trailer as hard as he could. He was going for broke on this one.

Back inside the trailer, Dwight sat shaking with terror, as it must have seemed to him that the Devil himself was coming for him. Pale white, Dwight grabbed his briefcase, opened the trailer door, and jumped outside—not stopping to even put his shoes on he sprinted through the sand with all his might. "You summoned the devil! You're a witch! You're evil!" Dwight yelled as he ran away from the trailer and from Wanda.

Waxer slowly rolled out from under the trailer as he watched Dwight's quick exit, and once the crazed man was far enough away, Waxer, still laughing, walked to the front door and looked in at his mother. He had never done anything like that before, and he didn't know how she was going to respond to it. He knew she was going to be angry but he'd had so much fun doing it, he was willing to take whatever punishment.

"Waxer! You know you just lost your mother a good customer?" Wanda said in Korean, still sitting at the table looking out at her son.

"He was a loser," Waxer answered back in the language of his mother.

"Yes, but he was truly a believer in the beyond. He was also 80 bucks a pop!"

Waxer reached inside the trailer door with his hand and grabbed his sleeping bag. "You got to admit it was pretty funny."

"Not funny! Not funny at all! You shouldn't put people down just because they might believe in something different than you!" Wanda continued, "You want me to fix you anything?" as Waxer opened the fridge and pulled out an apple and string cheese.

"Na, I ate at Lundon's," he said, moving to the patch of grass to spread his sleeping bag out.

"Do ya wanna try and reach Kevin tonight?" Wanda pushed.

"Mom!" Waxer yelled. "You know I don't believe in that stuff. Please leave me alone about Kevin and Jumper! I don't wanna think about them anymore today . . . or anymore ever!"

Waxer spread his sleeping bag out over the sand and then sat on top of it looking out over the water. He took a bite of his apple and after a moment he reached up with his hand and wiped the tears out of his eyes.

That very same evening, back in Lundon's house, Lundon sat at the kitchen table finishing her dinner. She could sense, because of the lack of conversation during the meal, that something was bothering her mom, and like always when something was bothering Sonia, Lundon wanted nothing more than to help make her feel better if she could.

"Momma? What's wrong?"

"Nothing," Sonia said, thinking deeply about whether to share her thoughts with Lundon or not. "Well, yes...I saw Daddy's old surfboard today and it..."

"You wanna talk to him?" Lundon asked, interrupting Sonia's statement.

"Later! When we say our prayers."

"No silly, not like that," Lundon giggled. "I mean down by the water. You can meet Sparkles."

"Who is Sparkles?" asked Sonia, not having any idea that it was another one of Lundon's 'sea' friends.

"She's a starfish. She comes every time I talk to Daddy."

"Lundon!" Sonia responded, realizing Lundon was again in her make-believe world. "You know I'm uncomfortable when you play around like this! Besides, you're starting to get too old to believe in such childish things!"

"Just come and see!" Lundon begged. "Please, Mom."

"There's no starfish!" Sonia snapped.

"You wanna make a little bet?" Lundon said with an 'I dare you' tone of voice.

"Okay! You're on!" Sonia said, knowing this was her chance to prove once and for all to Lundon that these things were not real. "But, young lady, if it's a no-show for the starfish, you have to promise you will stop all this nonsense!"

"Sparkles will show up! You'll see."

"No! I think it will be somebody else who sees," Sonia said with a warm grin.

Sonia was sure she finally had a way to help ease Lundon out of that crazy make-believe world she'd lived in for so long with her dad. Lundon, showing equally as much confidence in what she believed, jumped up from the table. She was more than ready to finally prove that the wonderful and magical world of the sea that she shared with her father did exist.

Sonia followed close behind Lundon, letting her lead the way. It didn't take them long to reach the surf as Lundon quickly found the spot she always used. She looked up at her mother, pleased, and then knelt down facing the water.

Sonia hesitated a moment, somewhat taken aback by Lundon's confidence. She knew, though, having come that far, she had to go all the way with the bet. She cautiously knelt down next to her daughter.

"Hi, Pops!" Lundon said, starting right into her routine. "Guess what? Someone really special wants to talk to you."

She looked up at her mother who still seemed unwilling to join in. "Well, go ahead; Sparkles won't come if you don't talk."

Sonia found her plan starting to backfire. Lundon's confidence was too solid, and besides, she hadn't expected she'd have to actually participate. She thought all she'd have to do was watch Lundon do her make-believe thing, listen to some excuse as to why the starfish didn't show up and that would be it.

Sonia hesitated a long time, looking down into the water, then up into the sky, then back again at Lundon, then back up into the sky. She knew then she was going to have to at least try and play along. Otherwise, her plan would not work for sure.

"Kevin?" Sonia finally said, still looking up at the sky.

"It's okay!" Lundon said, understanding her mother was new at this sort of thing. "But he's not up in the sky, silly! He's uh, down in the water. Remember?"

"Kevin?" Sonia said again, looking into the water. "I miss you . . . and . . . it's so hard being without you." She realized that it wasn't all that hard to do. Sonia looked at Lundon and winked. But before she continued, she noticed a very strange, transparent, pink reflection spreading out over a portion of the surf about 25-yards out moving toward them. Quick, menacing sounds rumbled up from under the surface but as suddenly as the pink color and eerie sounds had appeared, they were gone. It had happened so fast that Sonia didn't know for sure if she'd seen or heard anything, so she continued speaking to her missing husband, not comprehending what she had just witnessed. "Lundon has really grown up in these last three months. She is so happy to be out of school for the summer. She'll start junior high this fall. You'd be so proud of her."

"Oh, Pops? I'm making you a present," Lundon said, cutting into Sonia's conversation. "It's a bridge for you to come home on. Maybe I could take it to you."

Sonia really didn't like hearing that, and knew she was going to have to stop Lundon right then and there, but before she could get the words out, Lundon pointed at something.

"Look! It's Sparkles," Lundon announced as she reached down into the water and picked up the adorable little starfish.

Sonia couldn't believe her eyes.

"Hi, Lundon!" Sparkles said, as clearly as if Lundon had been speaking.

Sonia's eyes grew large as she stared at the little sea creature that was looking up at Lundon. Sonia had heard it speak but doubt immediately overpowered her mind—it was impossible for a starfish to speak and Sonia dismissed it as her mind playing tricks on her.

"Hi, Sparkles!" Lundon excitedly answered. "Look! My mom's here."

Sparkles turned her head to get a look at Sonia. At that very moment, an alarming pink flash of light coming from under the water thundered toward them. Sonia knew the light was real and assured herself her mind was not playing tricks.

"Oh, my! You must stay away from the ocean!" Sparkles warned in a serious but low whisper, as though she did not want someone or something else to hear. Sonya now believed the starfish was speaking and the words resonated inside her. "I can see you are both in great danger," said Sparkles with fear as she turned and jumped from Lundon's hand and back into the rising tide. Not understanding what was going on, Lundon stepped into the surf trying to retrieve the starfish. The very instant Lundon's foot touched the water, the same menacing sound and pink reflection, more pronounced and more violent in its appearance, darted directly toward her.

Sonia screamed and quickly reached out to pull Lundon back onto the sand, holding her close.

"Did you see? Did you?" Lundon screamed, excited that now her mother could and would believe.

"Don't ever get in the water again! Stay away from this ocean!" Sonia ordered, pulling Lundon out of the water and away from the danger.

Lundon was a little confused by how her mother had reacted to Sparkles and how she acted like the world was coming to an end, but still, all Lundon could think about was that she'd won the bet. Her mother would surely have to start believing if even just a little.

With how fast everything had happened Sonia wasn't sure what she had witnessed, but what she was absolutely sure of, was she didn't like it . . . not one bit.

Something Sonia had never shared with Lundon before, even though she'd always planned on sharing it someday, was that at the tender age of five, Sonia had almost drowned while swimming in the ocean, but was rescued by one of her favorite uncles who died saving her life.

Sonia had not been that close to the water until that night. Even though she lived right next to it, she spent her life ignoring the ocean's presence and avoiding its lure. Over the years she had become unconscious to its many sounds and its pungent, salty smell. It was as though it never existed as far as Sonia O'Malley was concerned.

Lundon was sound asleep as Sonia finished tucking her into her safe, warm bed. Sonia was still very confused and worried about what she had or hadn't seen out there in the surf that night. The images kept coming into her mind, and she knew she was going to have to deal with it somehow.

She walked over to Lundon's dresser where there was a photo of Kevin in a seashell frame. She stared at it for a long time, then, as though she had just gotten an idea, turned and exited the room.

As she entered the hallway, she stopped in front of the door to Kevin's den. Still not sure that she really wanted to do it, she reached up on top of the doorframe and found the key. She unlocked the small padlock on the door, a door that had not been opened since Kevin went missing; but she had seen enough that night that she felt she needed some answers before she could effectively deal with it—not only for herself, but for Lundon, as well.

Sonia hesitated for several moments before opening the door but then switched on the light and moved into the den, her eyes on Kevin's desk. She'd been in this little room thousands of times, yet this time she was afraid—afraid of what she would find and at the same time afraid of what she wouldn't find. The room looked the same, but somehow it was different. The closer she got to the desk, the more she felt she absolutely didn't want to find anything. Still she continued forward. As she reached the desk, she looked at the things Kevin had left on top of it. For a moment, she felt safe, like there really wasn't anything to be worried about after all. Cautiously she looked things over, and once she felt like she could touch anything, she reached down and opened the top drawer.

The very first thing she saw in the drawer was a large book. It was Kevin's journal. She pulled it out and opened it. After she flipped through several pages of scribbles and notes on various topics, she noticed a small drawing of a dolphin and other types of fish. *Many* other types, actually, and after being somewhat taken aback by how well Kevin could draw, she wondered why he had drawn them in the first place. *What were they to him? What were they to Lundon? Why hadn't she known he could draw that well? What else didn't she know about her husband? How bizarre this whole thing was becoming,* she thought.

A few more pages were turned and again, the thought ripped through her mind: *Had she really not known much about her husband, after all?* There were all these drawings and sketches. In some ways, it looked to Sonia as though Kevin had been working on a comic book rather than doing research. If that were true, then the whole fantasy for Lundon was nothing more than a comic book story he was writing. *Could that really be all he was up to?* she wondered.

Sonia started to feel more at ease and as she continued looking through his journal, she became more impressed than curious, until she flipped the page. At first she froze, afraid to even breathe. Then she pulled back a bit as the blood in her head rushed straight down to her feet, and the smile turned to an oval, chin-dropping, opened-mouth position of surprise and disbelief.

On that page was a sketch of Sparkles, the starfish she'd seen earlier that very night down at the beach with Lundon.

She realized these drawings were not cartoon characters after all. They were drawings of real sea creatures; and one of those sea creatures had warned her to stay away from the water—in plain English, to boot.

That wasn't all. Below the sketch was a handwritten note identifying Sparkles as King Pom's messenger to Kevin and Jumper.

No way! She thought as she slammed the book shut and in a dazed state of mind, backed out of the room. She couldn't erase the images she'd seen.

Once she was out in the hall, she closed the door tight—locking it again with the same padlock. She couldn't rid her mind of what she'd just seen. It felt to her that the whole world she had believed in was fading and a new make-believe world was emerging. *Was she going crazy? Was Lundon not just playing make-believe and Kevin wasn't really dead? It couldn't be true! It was impossible! But so was a talking starfish!* Fear and uncertainty were the only things she could feel running through her veins. For a moment she prayed she was only dreaming, and that nothing she had seen that night was real. But then she felt guilty for rejecting the make-believe because that would mean that Kevin was going to walk through her door again whenever his work was finished with Jumper, the talking dolphin scientist. It all made her dizzy.

Chapter 6

Sonia's Worst Nightmare

By mid-morning of the next day, Lundon O'Malley had only one more stick to add to her bridge. As she attempted to glue the last Popsicle stick into place, a Frisbee glided into her hand, knocking the glue bottle to the sand. Lundon grabbed her wrist as a sharp pain spread up her forearm, but within seconds, something worse caught her attention as she watched the glue ooze out from its bottle, mixing with thousands of little white grains of sand. As though nothing had happened, a teenage boy rushed over and picked up his Frisbee, unconcerned about Lundon or the damage he had caused to her project. He just grabbed his toy and ran back to join his friends.

At that same time, an elderly tourist couple walked up to Lundon. The man was carrying a large cake box lid full of seashells. He had a big belly that hung out over his baggy short pants. The woman looked much younger, but still, the rough life of a Louisiana swamp-person showed in every wrinkle on her face, and there were too many of them to count. They had watched the episode with the Frisbee and it was clear that the man didn't think the teenager was a very nice young man.

"You boys be mo' careful! You could'a hurt dis here youngun'!" he hollered in the direction where the boy had resumed his careless fun.

"What's it to ya, ol' man?" the boy shouted back, as he and his friends ran away to play farther down the beach.

"You all rat, darlin'?" the old man asked.

"He ruined my glue!" Lundon said, not sure of what she should do about it.

"My! Ain't dis somethin'?" the old man said as he noticed Lundon's Popsicle-stick bridge. "Look at dis, Ida! Dis li'l angel has gone 'n made somethin' outta Popsicle sticks."

"Why, Suga," Ida said as she sat down next to Lundon. "You really have done a beautiful job on dis bridge."

"It's for my dad," Lundon said, pleased that someone had noticed her handiwork.

"Oh, Wes! Did you hear dat? Da li'l doll's done made a present fer her papa."

Instinctively, Lundon glanced up toward the taffy shop. Sonia was busy with customers and had not yet noticed the two new people who had joined Lundon down on the sand.

"You sure have lots of shells," Lundon said as she looked into Wes's cake box.

"We're gonna be makin' a birthday present out of 'em fer our grandbaby," a proud Wes responded.

"She's gonna be ten. How old are you?" Ida asked.

"Thirteen."

"It's lookin' like yer gonna need a little more glue to finish dat dere bridge. Tell ya what..." Wes said as he stood up. "I got a bottle dat's almost empty. Dat oughtta do da trick. I'll be rat back."

Wes picked up his box of shells and headed for the parking lot, leaving Ida and Lundon sitting there on the sand. "What's yer name?"

"Lundon O'Malley."

"D'ya comes to da beach a lot?"

"Every day. I live here."

"Ya do? Dat's..." Ida started to say but Wes's voice interrupted.

"Ida?" Wes hollered from the parking area.

Ida and Lundon looked toward the parking lot located about 25-yards away from the sand where they were sitting. That particular lot allowed beachgoers to park right down close to where the action was; and for that reason, it was the most popular parking lot at that section of the beach. It was always full and you'd have to be an early comer to be able to park there.

Wes stood at the rear of his van rummaging through a large box of junk looking for some old bottle of glue.

What Lundon could not see from where she was sitting, were several small children bound, gagged and crammed up against the back of the cab inside Wes's van. Their eyes were full of tears and what you could see of their faces showed a group of really scared boys and girls.

"Where'd ya put dem dere glue bottles?" Wes hollered as his voice carried down to where Lundon and Ida sat.

"Blind ol' crawfish!" Ida said as she stood up and took Lundon's hand. "Come on, Lundon! Let's go get yer glue."

Lundon and Ida stood up and started walking toward Wes. Lundon, worrying only about her glue, had no idea what Wes and Ida were really up to. The thought of being kidnapped was the furthest thing from her mind.

Wes was still rummaging through the box when Ida and Lundon reached him. Instantly, and without any warning, not even changing the expression on his face, Wes grabbed Lundon, stuffing a rag into her mouth so she could not scream, and shoved her up into the rear of the van with the other children.

"Hey! What do you think you're doin'?" Waxer yelled, having seen the whole episode from across the parking lot. He was returning to the taffy shop after making his first delivery for the day. Within a second, he dropped the empty boxes he was carrying and jetted toward the van on his skateboard. Wes and Ida had no idea there was a witness to their crime and since Waxer was so far away, they couldn't have heard his voice, anyway.

Once Lundon was far enough inside the back of his van, Wes climbed in and started to bind Lundon's arms and legs with several pieces of thin rope. Lundon's screams were nothing more than muffled groans that could not be heard outside of the metal walls of that van. Even with the weakened cries of the other children, no one outside the confines of that van had any idea what fear lay within.

Wes, still not aware that Waxer was on to him, finished tying Lundon, and then climbed down out of the van, slamming the two large rear doors shut. He then headed for the driver's side of the van as Ida made her way to the passenger door. Within moments, the van pulled forward heading for the exit to the parking lot of the beach that Lundon had called her home from the day she was born.

Waxer, still on his skateboard, hot-dogged it even faster down a busy bicycle path, heading opposite the flow of bicyclers, joggers, rollerbladers and pedestrians. He skillfully handled his skateboard as he jumped curbs and sped past people on his way to the exit of the parking lot. He didn't know exactly what or how, but he knew he had to do something to help Lundon. He knew Kevin would expect it of him.

Lundon studied the faces of the two boys and three girls that had already been bound and gagged before her. She knew they were not from her part of the beach because she didn't recognize any of them. It had all happened so fast and so unexpectedly. She tried to get her bearings but couldn't. She was scared like she had never been before. Lundon had no idea what was in store for her and like the others, tried to brace herself the best she could without the use of her arms and hands, as the vehicle gained speed, it swerved right and left, throwing them from one side of the van to the other.

Waxer jumped a curb and flew up and then back down a small construction ramp, gaining even more momentum as he got closer to the escaping van. He was as hot on his skateboard as he was on the waves of the ocean. Few kids his age enjoyed both skateboarding and surfing, but Waxer loved the thrill of riding his boards, whether on concrete or on the rolling sea.

Reaching the exit first, Wes pulled the van out onto a side road, obviously heading away from the beach. As the van sped out of the parking lot, and thinking they were getting away scot-free, Wes and Ida began taking off their disguises.

Both were very skilled at disguises because they were not really old people at all; middle-aged, maybe, but not old, old people by any stretch of the imagination. Though they both looked much younger than they had in full disguise, they also both looked more hardcore and rugged down to the bone. A long, thick scar stretched down the side of Wes's ugly face and Ida, missing most of her teeth looked back at the kids through the open tarp separating the cab from the rear section of the van. A big, sickening grin exposed the remaining rotting teeth in her mouth.

Even as the van traveled farther down the small beachside road, Wes and Ida had absolutely no idea that a seventeen-year-old surfer kid was still hot on their tail. As far as they knew, no one was the wiser. Quiet in, fast out! That is how they worked and that is what they thought they were doing that day, too.

The two kidnappers sat back in their seats and tried to get comfortable as they prepared for the long haul with the children they had just collected from that day's beach run. As Wes made another turn, he looked into his side mirror just in time to see Waxer speeding off a bike trail and grabbing onto the rear fender of his van.

Wes, not a bit worried about the young intruder, reached down and pulled a snake from a small swamp-water tank that was on the floor, sloshing back and forth next to his seat. The snake wrapped itself around Wes's left arm as he grabbed the wheel with both hands and stepped down hard on the gas pedal.

"I'll kill dat kid! I'll kill him...."

"Who?" Ida asked. "What's goin' on?"

"Der's a punk dat wants ta die!" Wes responded with a mean look in his eye that matched the growl of his voice and the stench of his breath.

"Well, get rid of him, you stupid ol' maggot! He could mess everthin' up!"

Wes gave his wife a sour frown as he stepped on the gas again, swerving left and right, doing all he could to shake Waxer loose.

Waxer held on for all he was worth, just missing garbage cans, trees, and one or two telephone poles along the way.

In the back of the van, Lundon and the other children struggled to keep from being flung around the rear of the vehicle, as it swerved right and left over the small, one-way road. The children instinctively learned that if they bunched together, back to back, and pushed their legs up against the walls, they could hold on better with less danger of getting hurt.

At the same time that Lundon and the other children were being kidnapped, back down on the beach where Lundon's Popsicle-stick bridge rested in the sand, the surf, in a very strange manner, began to crawl up toward the bridge, and slowly engulfed it, pulling it out and away from the dry land into the deep water of the ocean. Only Kevin's dive bag remained, marking the spot on the sand where Lundon had spent the last moments on her beloved beach.

Waxer was still clutching onto the van, dodging every type of obstacle Wes could find along the way. Waxer's grip was getting weaker as he clung to the tail section. He was not sure if he could maintain his hold much longer.

"All rat...I'm a finished playin' wit dis here tough boy! Watch dis, big mouth!" Wes yelled, looking right into his wife's face as she squinted her eyes and held her nose from his stinky breath.

At that exact moment, Wes slammed on his brakes and opened his door. A fraction of a second later, Waxer crashed face-first into the open door, his skateboard shooting forward like a rocket being launched into space. Wes reached out and grabbed Waxer by the hair, peeling him off the door.

Stunned, Waxer found himself staring into the smelly face of Wes's pet swamp snake and before Waxer could gather his senses, he was added to the van's headcount. Not being far enough away from the beach, Wes didn't dare spend too much time gagging and binding Waxer; he just picked him up, tossed him into the back of the van, slammed the doors and sped off down the beachfront road away from the beach.

Lundon's Popsicle-stick bridge had floated far enough out to sea that no one standing on the beach could possibly see it. Suddenly, and from out of nowhere, the same pink color swirled up from beneath, engulfing it like wet, slimy fingers, slowly pulling it down under the water. Within moments, the only thing left was the one lone stick that had not been glued onto the structure, floating up and back with the movement of the ocean current.

Under the water, and like a falling feather from a bird's nest high up in a tree, the bridge floated down and rested on the sandy ocean floor. Once it had settled, the pink shade, almost like a school of transparent fish swimming in unison, pulled away and within a moment was gone.

Later that afternoon, most of the people had left the beach and the shops on the boardwalk were all starting to close for the day. Kevin's navy dive bag Lundon had brought with her down to the beach that day lay in a small puddle of seawater and the empty spilt glue bottle rested in the sand next to it.

A pair of legs approached the puddle and stopped. It was Sonia looking down at the dive bag. She was confused as to where Lundon might be and why she had abandoned her things. Sonia knew Lundon had wandered off before but she'd never ever left her bag of toys behind. She quickly turned to a couple who were preparing their things to leave, and asked them if they had seen a little girl around that area. They had not.

Sonia frantically moved from couple to couple, group to group, and no one had seen any child, boy or girl, playing there alone for hours.

In her mind it seemed to Sonia that it hadn't been more than thirty minutes or so since she had looked down from the taffy shop and seen Lundon gluing her sticks together. *How could these people say they hadn't seen any children around for hours? It hadn't been hours, had it?* Sonia thought, as her heart pounded harder and faster. *Where had her mind been? It had been a bit busy at the shop, but...had it really been hours?* Her mind was running in overdrive and she couldn't catch her breath. She started to panic but knew she had to pull herself together and find her daughter. She wasn't going to let her mind play crazy games. *No!* She knew that there was only one thing to do and that was to find her daughter and find her fast.

"Okay, Sonia," she said out loud. "Only real questions! Nothing more!" *Real questions? How long had Lundon been gone? That was a real question, wasn't it? How long would Lundon leave her things unattended? When was the last time she'd remembered actually seeing Lundon? Had it really only been thirty minutes? One hour? Four hours? Longer?*

Sonia took deep breaths, trying to keep herself from losing control. She looked up toward her home, and it was then, in that one instant, she felt an easy calm come over her.

Of course! Lundon had to use the bathroom and couldn't hold it. That was as good an answer for why Lundon would have left her things as anything Sonia could think of. *When you really gotta go,* she thought, *you do things that you normally wouldn't.* "Like leaving a treasured dive bag of her father's on the sand, unattended," she said, finishing her thoughts with words coming out of her mouth.

Sonia felt better and after picking up the empty glue bottle and dive bag, she instinctively headed off in the direction of her small beachfront home. The closer she got, the faster her pace increased. By the time she reached the house, she was practically in a dead sprint. "Lundon? Lundon O'Malley!" Sonia yelled out as she entered the house, and hurried toward the bathroom. Lundon was not there. Sonia walked to Lundon's bedroom. "Oh, please be in here..." she begged, sticking her head into the room.

It was empty. Sonia, in a near-trance state, gazed at the floor, and after a few numbing moments, realized she was staring down at the few unused Popsicle sticks lying on the rug next to Lundon's bed.

Suddenly a frightening thought pierced Sonia's mind, and a bolt of fear shot through her body as she recalled the words Lundon muttered while she was down at the surf the night before talking to her dad and telling him about the bridge she was making for him.

"Oh, no! Lundon! You didn't try and take that bridge to your dad, did you?" screamed Sonia. Dropping the dive bag and glue bottle to the floor, she darted out of the bedroom, heading back outside—out to face her biggest and scariest enemy: the sea.

Her heart still pounding with fear, Sonia finally reached the surf. *If only the fantasy hadn't been allowed to go on for so long,* she thought to herself as she looked into the water. And, as if she knew exactly what she would find, she spotted the lone Popsicle stick that was floating back and forth in the shallow waves close to shore.

Instantly, the worst of her fears flooded her mind—her heart—and she couldn't hold it inside any longer. "Dios mio! No! Lundon!" She screamed out at the rumbling waves as they came in and out flaunting the vastness of the open sea. Then, from the dark underbody of the boardwalk a strange and taunting sound grew louder and more menacing, as though it were beckoning her to come closer.

Not hesitating, Sonia turned and ran into the darkness, hoping—praying—that somehow, Lundon would be there, safe and all right, waiting for her mommy to come and take her home.

"Lundon! Lundon!" Sonia screamed as she reached the core of the darkness, where gigantic black tar-soaked pillars sprang up from the sand, like towering elephant legs supporting the vastness of the large boardwalk resting on top of them. Sonia called out for Lundon several more times and then, realizing Lundon was not there either, fell to her knees in a crazed, delirious state of confusion as the sound of the ocean pierced her eardrums, screeching and taunting its threats. Then, as before, the surf began changing into a haunting pink apparition as it swelled up and wrapped itself around the pillars, roaring its mocking sounds, laughing at Sonia.

"No! No!" Sonia screamed as she picked herself up off the sand.

Hearing Sonia's screams, the large violent wave became angry, and it roared wildly as it crashed into the pillars, coming closer and closer to the terrified woman.

Sonia braced herself and prepared for a fight, realizing she was not just facing a wave, but something that was alive. "What do you want with my daughter?" Sonia screamed. "Who are you?"

As though it had been waiting for Sonia to ask that very question, the large wave morphed into a giant pink jellyfish—a female pink jellyfish. Then it rolled forward, and, like a charging bull, crashed through the pillars toward Sonia ready to crush its prey.

As it reached Sonia, she swung and kicked at it, not willing to give an inch. "Give me back my baby!"

"Never! She's mine!" retorted the jellyfish wave as it theatrically swirled and wrapped itself around the gigantic pillars like it was the villain in a ballet. With mocking laughter, it sneered at Sonia as it moved ever closer.

"I won't let you do this! I won't!" Sonia cried out as she swung her fists at the wave.

The wave suddenly stopped, becoming very still, frozen right in front of Sonia's face; then, throwing a large burst of water in the shape of a huge fist, knocked Sonia to the ground, unconscious.

"Your kind caused the death of my husband and my child, so I've taken yours!" the enormous wave roared in a voice that shook the whole pier to its core.

Sonia lay there still and motionless on the wet sand as the crazed jellyfish wave, laughing hysterically, withdrew back into the surf and disappeared. The only thing left remaining under that dark, lonely pier was a rhythmic set of waves swishing gently up and back against Sonia's limp body.

The sign on the freeway showed that Wes's van was heading out of Florida, moving north and then west towards New Orleans. In the rear of the vehicle, Lundon sat quietly watching and listening. The other five children were huddled together against the other wall, and were really, really scared. Waxer was sitting alone by the rear doors. He looked more angry than frightened, but at least he was not bound and gagged like the others, and was in a position to help Lundon and the others if the chance presented itself.

The tarp between the cab and the rear section was pulled open, allowing Wes and Ida to keep their eyes on their captives. Ida was driving as Wes slept. His snake, though, was coiled and resting on his shoulder facing the children as the van vibrated like a smooth-running lawnmower moving northward. As Ida sipped some coffee and munched on a sandwich, of course not sharing any with the children, she noticed several blinking lights up ahead on the road. It first looked like an accident but soon she was able to see it was actually a police roadblock. She started to slow down as she reached over to wake Wes by digging her nails into his leg.

"Wes! Wes! Look on up der! Da poleese! Dey be stoppin' everyone."

The word 'police' reverberated extra loudly in Waxer's ears as his eyes grew large and his heart beat with fear and anticipation. He sat up straight and tilted his head to the left trying to get in the best position he could to hear everything.

Wes sat up and peered out through the window, trying to get an idea of what was going on. There were Highway Patrol officers stopping each car.

"One peep outta ya and yer goners!" Wes warned as he reached up and pulled the heavy tarp down, shutting the kids inside the now pitch-black back part of the van.

The children sat there frozen, dreading what might happen next.

"Good evening to y'all tonight," said one of the patrolmen as he stuck his head closer to the driver's side window of the van. "We're out warning everyone headed north that there's been reports of huge killer wasps in the area. There are several different swarms of the critters raising all kinds of raucous. So keep your windows up. Do not stop or get out of your vehicle for the next 100 miles."

"Yes, sir!" Ida said in a friendly manner as she hurried to roll the window up. "Dank you officer; we do dat!"

Waxer faced the front of the van. He knew he'd have to scream out then or forever hold his peace. Just as he opened his mouth to cry for help, the tarp jerked back enough for Wes to peep through. He stared right at Waxer with a look that would paralyze anyone. Waxer sat there with his mouth wide open but did not dare make a sound. He knew that he'd been busted and that his chance to scream out for help was lost and he slowly closed his mouth. Seconds later the van started moving and within the time it took for Waxer to start breathing again, they were well away from any hope of being rescued.

Lundon continued to stare at Waxer, almost as if she stared hard enough and long enough he'd get the hint and hurry and do something about this whole situation. He knew, though, that as long as they were in that van, he would not have much of a chance to do anything. He was going to have to wait for a better chance once they arrived at their new destination, whatever and wherever that might turn out to be.

Knowing that Wes must be feeling like he and is wife were safe from getting napped for kidnapping, Waxer thought it might be the best time to whisper something to Lundon. He hadn't noticed Wes peeking back through the slit in the tarp for the last several minutes. He quietly slid closer to her and carefully tapped her with his foot.

Lundon sat quietly as he placed his mouth close to her ear. "I can't do anything while we're in this piece of junk prison," Waxer whispered. "Once we are out of here, I'll try to find a way for us to escape, so don't do anything stupid! Do you understand?" Lundon knew he was right and anyway, she was too afraid to do anything, stupid or otherwise. She nodded her head.

Convinced that she will do as he said, Waxer moved back and leaned against the cold metal of the rear doors.

Back in Florida under the pier, Sonia laid unconscious on the ground, like a rag doll that had fallen off a moving wagon and slumped on top of the cool sand. As she finally came to, there was no way for her to know how long she'd been there.

Slowly she opened her eyes and lifted her head off the wet ground, struggling to remember how and why she was there in the first place. Feeling dizzy, she sat up and tried to gather her bearings. As her eyes focused, she noticed the beach area just outside from where she was sitting; the spot where Lundon had last sat and played. The surf in front of her was gently moving back and forth without any evidence of the violence she had experienced earlier.

Instantly she remembered everything: losing Lundon, the wave, the jellyfish, and, of course, the fight. She jumped up and ran down into the water kicking and screaming at the slow, soft, breaking waves.

"I hate you! You evil witch! I'm not going to let you hurt us anymore! I won't...," Sonia cried out as two arms suddenly wrapped around her from behind, lifting her up and out of the water. Startled, Sonia screamed, kicked, and scratched as wildly as she could, thinking that the jellyfish wave had returned to finish the job.

"Sonia! Calm down," the voice cried out. "It's me, Rolley. It's okay...it's okay."

Sonia realized who it was and reached her arms up, clinging onto him. Then the reality hit her that Lundon was really gone, and within just a few short seconds, totally brokenhearted and defeated, she began crying uncontrollably. Without the strength to stand on her own, she collapsed in Rolley's arms.

Never in her entire life had Sonia believed that a person could hurt as much as she did; first for the loss of her husband, and now the loss of her only child, her baby, her friend, her daughter. Sonia's pain was greater than anything she'd ever imagined.

Early the next morning, after what seemed like a lifetime to the children, Wes's van approached a very desolate area around the swamplands of New Orleans. The road was narrow and unpaved, and after a few bumpy turns, the van pulled through a wide gate designed in the shape of a large butterfly.

Bordering both sides of the gate were thick bushes that stretched to the top of the fence. Because it was so high, it was impossible to see inside the walls of what seemed to be very spacious grounds. Once the van was inside, and the gates were closed, anyone inside the yard was also prevented from seeing what was outside. The place was very private and protected—a virtual fortress.

A small parking area was next to the open grounds of the estate. Green grass and shrubs of every kind surrounded the grounds. There were two or three huge playground areas with rides and playthings everywhere, and at the far side of the spacious yard sat a white house—a mansion. The property looked like a carnival built for the very wealthy. Everything was clean and the colors were bright and assorted. It was an extremely happy place by the looks of it. The only thing out of place was the netting which stretched high over the entire property. It was the kind of a net you'd see in a bird sanctuary or a golf driving range.

Still locked inside the van, hungry and tired, the children sat wondering what was going to happen next. Suddenly, and without any warning, the rear doors flung open and as the children looked out, the stabbing pain of the bright sunlight temporarily blinded each of them.

Waxer pulled back to the far corner, trying to hide the best he could. He expected that Wes would reach to grab him, but to his, and the other children's surprise, there was no Wes. Instead, there appeared a transparent image of a beautiful woman standing in the doorway staring in at them. At first, all they could make out was a soft pinkish haze that surrounded the woman, but after a few moments the children's eyes grew more accustomed to the sunlight and they could see the woman's face, and unlike Wes's and Ida's, hers radiated love and kindness. The beautiful pink dress she wore moved as if there were a gust of wind encircling her at all times. She emitted a bright glow that made the children feel warm and comfortable around her. Her name was Dalina, and she was head mistress of this wondrous estate.

Dalina gently reached in and helped the children out of the van, removing the remaining bands binding their hands and feet, caressing them, and trying to show them that they were no longer in any danger.

"Everything will be all right now," Dalina said as she continued making the children feel welcome. "You don't need to be afraid anymore, children. You've come to your Fairy Godmother's Butterfly Wonderland Home of Happiness."

The children were amazed as they viewed the massive yard around them. It was warm, fun and designed to satisfy every interest of playful, young children.

Finally, Dalina reached for the last child, helping her step out into the sunlight. When she looked into Lundon's eyes, she became very excited; she had been waiting a long time for that particular child to arrive.

"Lundon?" the woman softly asked.

Lundon didn't say anything; she just nodded her head in an affirmative motion.

"I've been waiting for you. I'm so happy you're here."

Lundon couldn't help but notice Dalina's obvious joy. She acted as though she knew Lundon and welcomed her like she was greeting her long-lost niece. Lundon couldn't understand what the overbearing attention meant. She gently pulled away from Dalina and joined the other children all grouped together a few feet away.

Wes and Ida walked into view from around the front of the van. The children pulled closer together; obviously very afraid of the cruel and mean man and woman who had taken them from their homes—from their lives that must have seemed a million miles away, maybe even more.

Miss Hope, one of Dalina's helpers, stepped out in front of the children, as though she was trying to protect them from Wes and Ida. She gently led them away toward the big, beautiful, white, two-story mansion that sat upon a small knoll covered with the greenest grass Lundon had ever seen.

Lundon couldn't figure any of it out. Nothing made any sense to her. She looked back over her shoulder as Miss Hope led them away from Dalina, Wes and Ida. She tried to see where Waxer was. She couldn't understand why he hadn't been helped out of the van along with the rest of them. Lundon wanted to call out for him but was afraid that Wes would hurt him if she did.

Maybe they forgot about Waxer. Maybe he'll be able to escape and somehow come and rescue us, Lundon thought to herself. New hope filled her mind as she followed the woman and the other children away from the parking area.

"Where's dat boy?" Wes snarled after he realized Waxer was not with the group of kids that had been taken away.

Dalina wondered what he was talking about as Wes quickly moved to the rear door of the van and jerked it open to look inside. At that exact moment, Waxer darted out from the shadows and jumped toward the front of the van. Once he got halfway over the front seat, though, Wes's snake suddenly popped up, greeting Waxer for the second time, face-to-face.

Waxer looked at Wes, then back into the face of the hissing snake. Instantly changing plans, Waxer jumped down off the seat and out the side doors, going for the tall fence a few yards away.

Just before he got halfway up the eight-foot wall, Wes's grubby old hands grabbed him and pulled him down, dragging him by his hair back toward Dalina.

"I'm a gonna kill dis boy, I swea' I'll kill dis one!" Wes growled as he stopped in front of Dalina.

"What's this?" asked Dalina. "Another troublemaker?"

"We had no choice. He saw us takin' the last youngun'," Ida explained.

"You know where we keep the troublemakers!" Dalina snarled in an ice-cold manner, very unhappy about the uninvited guest. "Take him to the cellar and leave him—unharmed, mind you. He should make a great soldier."

Wes and Ida walked off in a different direction than Lundon and the other kids had been taken. Dragging Waxer with them Ida stopped after a few yards and shouted back at Dalina.

"What about da money? Dis makes tree trips. You best be a payin' today! You don't wanna learn how swamp people is when dey be angry!"

"Take him to the cellar and leave him, I said. I'll have your pay and a very special bonus waiting for you after you finish with the boy," Dalina said as she waved off the two grungy swamp-landers.

"I told ya I'd be geddin' a bonus outta dat woman, didn't I?" Ida whispered, leading both Waxer and Wes toward a very large building with a huge door that was also shaped like a butterfly.

The estate was a place any kid would love to come and visit. It looked like there was no end to the toys and the playgrounds. It would take a kid several days to enjoy each of the rides alone. With the exception of how the children were brought there, the place seemed like a pretty nice joint. Most kids could really get used to it—maybe never even want to leave.

Chapter 7

Going Off the Deep End

"Come on..." Rolley answered in disbelief as he sat on the floor in Sonia's front room desperately trying to understand what Sonia was telling him.

"No, please hear me out. I fought fist to fist with a giant wave—a giant wave that turned into a jellyfish," Sonia said as she sat on her sofa trying to make him understand what she had experienced.

Rolley shut his eyes and lowered his head, not wanting to hear anymore.

"It spoke to me. It told me it would never give Lundon back to me. She...it, said that my kind had killed her child and husband, or something like that."

"I think this is all about you not being able to find Lundon," Rolley said, still trying to make sense out of the whole deal. "Look, the police asked you to wait until after meeting with him before filing a report. This will give you a chance to get some rest, and a chance to change these ridiculous thoughts before tomorrow."

"No! Listen, before that..." Sonia continued, refusing to be swayed from the reality of her experience. "Lundon and I had gone down to the surf to talk to Kevin. There was a starfish I heard speak...and that pink jellyfish tried to get at Lundon then. Believe me! That jellyfish wave has my baby! Might even have Kevin, for all I know."

Rolley leaned back and took a deep breath. He had always thought that Sonia was the most sensible of the O'Malleys, but still he could understand where she was coming from, at least somewhat. With his experience that fatal night several months ago, with the talking Muck Munchers and dolphins, he wasn't ready not to believe it but wasn't ready to believe it either.

"Sonia! Please don't tell these kinds of stories to anyone else, especially not the cops. I'll do what I can to help you find Lundon, but you've got to keep these things just between us. This stuff has to stay our little secret, okay?"

Sonia sat there thinking about what Rolley was saying. She wasn't sure what to think or feel anymore, and that was becoming a big problem for her. She had always been proud of herself in regard to her down-to-earth, commonsensical approach to how and what she thought about things in her life. She was very practical in her beliefs, but now she wasn't sure if what she had always thought to be real was nothing more than pure fantasy. Or, was she simply going crazy?

Dalina's office, located in the back section of her spacious mansion, was modern and elaborately decorated, with ceramic sea-life figurines everywhere. Behind her desk was a submarine-style hatch door.

Dalina stepped into her office and closed the door, locking it behind her. She danced toward her desk, picked up a remote control and clicked on some upbeat music. She faced a large mirror and in a theatrical manner pulled off her wig, all in beat with the music. She was totally bald, with pale, pink, translucent skin.

As she moved behind a fabric-covered screen to change her clothes, she began 'talk-singing' about the very thing that had made her so happy. "Today, today, a day so grand...the power to stay on this dirty old land...has just fallen into the palm of this nonhuman hand."

As she continued talk-singing, she threw parts of her clothing up into the air as they, in rhythm to the music, floated down to the floor in front of the screen. She then moved out from behind it, dressed in a beautiful pink nightgown and waltzed back to the hatch door.

"I am Dalina, Queen of the Sea. Now I can destroy all that threatens us, you will see. But first, Lundon O'Malley must love and believe in only me."

Dalina opened the hatch door and looked down into the sunken room that was filled with seawater. As she dove in, and as her human body went deeper and deeper into the tank, she metamorphically turned into her original self, that of a beautiful pink jellyfish queen, Queen Dalina.

As she changed form, Kevin O'Malley's image emerged from her body and floated for a moment next to her, like a mirage of his human form, and then within an instant, it broke up into a million little particles that quickly floated up to the top of the water above her head.

"The Fairy Godmother is not really me, you see! No! No! No! It's only Lundon's daddy, under my spell and magically controlled by me, and once Lundon and her mother both believe he is dead, much like the others, he'll be my puppet for all eternity."

As Dalina reached the bottom of the tank, she landed on top of her seashell bed. Her tentacles covered every inch of the bed as she lay her head down, smiling to herself over the successful capture of Lundon O'Malley, the daughter of the very man who was giving her the power to survive on land.

Down in the dark, dingy cellar where Dalina kept troublemakers was a slow-moving crab creature that made its way over several unidentifiable skeletons. Six inches of seawater covered the bottom of this scary, damp and moldy underground jail cell.

Waxer was huddled over in one corner, leaning against a cinderblock wall. He was cold and scared and wondered why he and he alone had been put down in that isolated place.

The room was small, as far as underground cellars went, and the only light was the sunlight that made its way through six or seven small holes in the cinderblock wall that were higher than even a tall man could reach without a stepladder. The openings were four or five inches wide and the same basic height. They were not exactly round, but somewhat so. They looked like someone had bashed big spaces in the wall with a hammer. They were big enough for snakes and rats to crawl through or maybe a small bird, but definitely not a human boy.

The ceiling was wood with a hatch door that locked from the outside. Directly under that door was an old, rickety, wooden staircase. It looked just slightly larger than a handmade stepladder with four steps from top to bottom.

Waxer wondered where Lundon had been taken, and if she was safe and warm or cold and scared. He knew he had to try and do something to save her—to save himself—but how? As he thought of these things, he began to study the place over, looking for a way to escape.

Sonia, Wanda, and Rolley were sitting in a detective's office at the police department listening to one very frustrated cop. Sonia was not at all happy about what that policeman was trying to tell her.

"I understand that," the detective argued, "but I have no choice. I cannot justify the manpower it would require to send a search team out to cover that entire section of the ocean. If you had one piece of evidence, then...but from what I can see here, there is just no evidence that your daughter drowned."

"What about the Popsicle stick floating on the water?" Sonia argued as her eyes showed the intense frustration she was feeling.

"That could have been anyone's stick."

"What about Lundon saying she was going to take the bridge to her father? She believes her daddy is alive down there, I tell you!"

"Let's quit wasting time," the detective spouted back in a strong enough voice to let Sonia know he wasn't going to be made a fool of, but caring enough not to step on a wounded mother's heart. "I'm going to include Lundon's case with the five missing children from that same day...six if we count Warner."

Sonia stood up and walked to the window, taking a deep breath. "There's more..."

"Sonia, please!" Rolley begged, knowing exactly where she was going to take the conversation.

"No!" Sonia responded, looking right into Rolley's eyes, and then back at the detective. "I didn't just collapse under the pier that day. I fought, fist-to-fist, with a giant jellyfish wave..."

The detective really didn't want to hear any more, and the expression on his face clearly indicated as such, wounded mother or not.

"It talked! It told me..."

"Stop!" The detective shouted, holding his hands up into the air. "Don't you say another word...next!"

Rolley motioned for Sonia to be quiet, and to his big surprise, she did. She even sat back down in her chair.

"Wanda Worthington?"

"Yes?" Wanda answered.

"It says here you're not sure if Warner is missing or not. When did you see him last?"

"Oh...I don't know. A few days maybe. We call him Waxer!"

"A few days. Well, where do you think he is then?" the detective asked again in a sarcastic tone as he scribbled the name 'Waxer' next to Warner Worthington. "Warner Waxer Worthington," he mumbled to himself, trying to subdue a smile as he looked up at Wanda to see why she had not answered his question.

Wanda had laid several tarot cards down on top of the detective's desk. He knew right then and there that he was dealing with not one, but two of the weirdest women ever to grace his office—and at the same time.

"These cards say he will soon be in the wind," Wanda said as she glanced up from the cards and stared directly into the blood-shot eyes of a very bewildered detective.

"What is that supposed to mean?" questioned the detective, becoming increasingly agitated.

"I'm not sure yet. If he does not come home tonight…I'll try…how'd you say…astro-projection, you know, and enter his body. I'll let you know more tomorrow."

"Please! Please! No need to do that! Just have someone call me if he comes home," the detective said, as he popped a handful of aspirin, and gulped an entire cup of cold coffee to wash them down. He then turned his questioning back to Sonia.

"Mrs. O'Malley? You said Waxer never came back after taking out a delivery. Is that right?"

"His surfboard is still there at the taffy shop."

"And how long after Waxer left for the delivery did you notice Lundon missing?"

"I'm not sure; about an hour...maybe longer," Sonia answered.

"All right! I have no choice but to surmise all seven children have been kidnapped, possibly by the same person or persons. I'll inform you if there are any further developments. Thank you for all your...uh...help."

The detective stood up and happily escorted the group out of his office. He was finished and didn't want to listen to even one more word of weirdness.

The very next day, outside in the spacious yard of the Butterfly Wonderland School of Happiness, were dozens of children. The kids were all being watched over by several helpers as they played together and were all dressed in colorful fun new outfits.

There were also several adult men working here and there around the yard. To the children, the men were just gardeners or groundskeepers, but for Dalina's purposes, they were extra security to help squelch a problem should one arise, and, of course, to help her if any of the kids decided to try and run off. The men were all dressed in white uniforms.

Next to the larger rides were slides, swings, sandboxes, and every type of plaything for the children to enjoy. The children were divided into three groups; each group separate from the other.

The first group, called the Butterflies, was the children who had been there for a long time and had pretty well forgotten their old lives. Those children were the most comfortable and were having the majority of the fun.

They were all wearing very strange looking backpacks that were strapped onto them much like a parachute harness, but once they began running, the backpack morphed into part of their actual body taking on the color and texture of the kid's shirt or blouse, and after the kids gained enough speed, wings shot out, and within moments they began to fly all around the yard, screaming and playing air-tag with their fellow fliers. Some of the older children even dared to fly up to the large netting that stretched over the entire length of the yard, keeping them inside like a net covering a bird sanctuary at your local zoo. Landing on the ground and slowing down to a walk caused the wings to morph into the backpack and the child could remove it like a real backpack.

Needless to say, the Butterfly group had the full run of most of the yard, and there were fewer people supervising them and those that were there to keep watch had their own backpacks strapped on so if need be, they too could fly up and untangle a winged child who got too close to the netting.

Then there were the Cocoons. They were the children who had not quite gotten with the program yet. They were still being talked to at every turn. They had helpers teaching and working with them, helping them to forget, prodding them to let go of the memory of their mothers and fathers—memories of their past lives. They were all constantly encouraged to have fun like the children in the Butterfly group. Some of the children in the Cocoon group played a little, moped a little, then played some more. Each step took them closer to losing their belief in and love for their parents—closer to being totally under Dalina's control. The average time under Dalina's control for kids in this group ranged from one week to several weeks. Each child had a different breaking point, depending on their own resolve and inner strength and of course, family history.

Lastly, there were the children like Lundon who had not been there much time at all, one or two days, maybe a week. They stayed to themselves or were with a helper constantly talking to them. In the first phase of reprogramming their lives, they were called the Caterpillars.

Dalina approached from the mansion, and just as she had the night before in her office, she walked in a very theatrical, showy manner, playing with the kids along the way, until she reached Lundon's group. Her silk dress waved in her own wake as she walked, and she was always smiling, and working to make the children feel more at ease.

"Hello, my darlings. Did you enjoy the cookies and ice cream you had for breakfast?" she asked, carefully looking each child over, checking for a response. "You are going to love it here. See the children with the butterfly wings on their backs? Well, they've learned how to have fun. In a few days some of them graduate to the big kids' fun house. After you earn your wings, you can play in that special, exciting place, too. Even though it's so much fun here, it is much, much, much more fun there."

The children had different reactions. Some seemed to be okay about what they'd heard, while some were slightly bothered, and yet others were still frightened and upset.

Lundon sat there with a blank look in her eyes, refusing to listen, refusing to even think of a new life away from Sonia and the beach.

"Where's Waxer?" Lundon defiantly asked, trying to show Dalina that she still remembered everything.

"Do you know it was your mothers and your fathers who sent you to me?" Dalina asked, ignoring Lundon's question outright. "It's true! They want you to learn how to live the fun life. Think about it! Isn't it true that your moms and dads never had enough time for you? Didn't they act like you always got in their way?"

Lundon could hear the words coming from Dalina's mouth, but she couldn't understand how they related to her in any way, shape or form. It all seemed unreal as she sat there and tried really hard not to listen. She had never, not once in her life, felt like she was in Sonia or Kevin's way. As a matter of fact, she knew without a question that her parents loved and adored her, 24 hours a day, 7 days a week and 365 days a year.

Still, unrelenting and ignoring Lundon, Dalina continued with her nonstop brainwashing efforts. "They would always be telling you to go play somewhere else, right? Well, this is the somewhere else they wanted you to be."

More and more of the children in Lundon's group started nodding their heads, as they began to agree with the poisonous words the beautiful woman in front of them was speaking.

"Lundon," Dalina said, directing her words right at Lundon. "Your mother sent you here because she wants me to help you to understand that your daddy is really dead, and that you will never see him again. She told me she wanted you to forget all those silly stories you believe in. She just wants you to play and have fun like other children."

Dalina's level of knowledge about Lundon's life confused Lundon. She wondered how it was possible Dalina knew so much about her. She tried her best to ignore Dalina, but this strange woman seemed to understand too much, which left a stinging feeling inside Lundon's mind—inside her heart, too. Dalina's knowledge about Lundon's family, more than her words, began to haunt Lundon.

"Soon," Dalina continued as she smiled at each of the children, "you will all be having tons of fun. So, let's get started. I have a brand new game for us to play. Who wants to play?"

Playing was the furthest thing from Lundon's mind, but many of the other kids in her group were starting to show signs they wanted to do more than sit around and be afraid.

Despite the fact that Lundon, and all of the children for that matter, had been kidnapped, there was absolutely no sign of danger anywhere around them; and all the helpers, even Dalina, seemed to be caring, friendly, and loving people.

With the exception of Lundon, Dalina knew she had that new group of Caterpillars right where she wanted them. These kids were going to be a cinch. Maybe even the easiest she's had since coming onto land from her kingdom under the sea.

By now, more than four days had passed by since Lundon had been kidnapped and Waxer, still down in the dark cellar, was working hard at scraping the mortar out of the seams separating two blocks of the cinderblock wall with his shark's tooth necklace. The mortar was old and since it was in a damp place, it was possible to scrape away with a sharp tool. Waxer had already bared one section about one inch into the gap between the two blocks, leaving a long, opened gap. He then moved up to the topside of the block and started digging at the upper portion. It was obvious that he intended to remove the heavy block so he could escape his dungeon.

While Waxer was hard at work and not concentrating on anything but his escape route, the door to the cellar loudly opened and a man hurried down the wooden steps and right up to where Waxer was working. Waxer didn't have enough time to stop scraping, let alone hide what he was doing.

Startled, Waxer tried the best he could to keep his back against the wall, hoping to hide his handiwork, as he found himself gazing up into the face of the scariest looking man he'd ever laid eyes on.

The man's name was Wart, and he was one of Dalina's helpers. He was carrying a small tray with one slice of bread and a bowl of water. It was Waxer's meal.

Wart's clothes fit him very well, tailored for his unique shape, with the shirt and pants pressed like a policeman's uniform. His face was badly scarred and thick black hair grew wildly all over his face, even on the tip of his nose, but there was not even one strand of hair on the poor man's head. His skin was rough and hard like worn leather on an old baseball glove, and his back sported a bloated hump larger than his head.

Wart handed the tray to Waxer, and then he looked up at the wall next to Waxer's head. Waxer was sure he'd been caught red-handed. And to add to Waxer's fears, Wart stared down at the wall as though he had noticed Waxer's work for sure. Wart pushed Waxer's head to one side, so as to get a better look. The deep gap that Waxer had been working on was now visible, but lucky for Waxer, Wart was not looking at that. Instead, he reached up and snatched a small crab creature that had crawled up to eye level, six inches or so away from Waxer's work area. Wart, acting like he'd just found a piece of chocolate candy, grabbed it and popped it into his mouth, eating it alive.

Waxer expected the worst as Wart finished chewing his crab snack. Wart then looked right into Waxer's face and smiled, turned and started to leave, not looking back again at the wall area. Before he reached the steps, Wart looked down at the water-covered floor and, bending down, snatched two more creatures in his hand.

"I know it's the same food fer ya everday," Wart said as he looked up at Waxer. "Bread and water's all she'll let me give ya!" He looked back down at his goodies he'd just caught. "If you start on any of these critters, just make sure you save a few each day fer me!"

The old man looked back at Waxer, grinned again and walked up and out of the cellar.

Waxer couldn't believe how close he'd come to getting caught. He glanced at the bread and water that Wart had brought for him to eat. He was so famished that the bread and water was starting to actually look like real food. He couldn't remember ever being that hungry before in his life.

The next day, out in the yard, some of the children in the Cocoon group were now playing more, and some of them were proud and excited to be receiving their butterfly wings from some of the female staff members.

Some of the children who had been in the Butterfly group from before were being promoted to the next, very secret level. They stood in single file, and were being led away from the playground area, walking toward a beautiful gate at the far side of the yard. The gate was the entrance to a big yellow building, the very building, in fact, that Waxer had been dragged into by Wes and Ida. Strangely, this building was the only building on the property that did not sit under the high netting.

As some of the children got close to the butterfly-shaped doorway, they turned and waved to some of their friends who were standing around the edge of the yard watching them being promoted.

The lure of what was in that big yellow building drew more and more of the children to dream of going into it themselves. To some of the kids, it seemed to be nothing but magical. Even though they knew that a promotion to the new level meant they'd never be seen in the general playground areas again, they didn't seem to mind at all. Actually they would never be seen anywhere around there again; not the house, not the dining hall or even the bedrooms.

Each one of those children knew that they were special and that Dalina loved them very much—they were being rewarded for being good and for listening to everything Dalina and her helpers told them. They were no longer concerned with their past lives; in fact, some didn't even *want* to remember at all. The time and fun that Dalina was giving them was all that mattered.

Like an old mother hen, Dalina stood waiting for the children to gather around the large butterfly-shaped doors.

"Now children," Dalina said with the same cheerfulness and radiance that always spread across her face. "Do you love your Fairy Godmother?"

"Yes, Fairy Godmother," each of the obedient children answered, almost in perfect unison.

"Come, my children! Your new adventures are waiting just inside," Dalina said, as she opened the doors. "Here we go."

The children pushed and shoved, and could not wait to get inside the building to see what was waiting just for them. As the last child entered, Dalina, still outside the building, looked back at the other children in the yard—waved, then whirled around and joined the group inside, shutting the big doors behind her.

Chapter 8

An Army of Insects

Most of the mortar had been scraped away from the block Waxer had been working on, but he wasn't near that wall. Instead, he was crouched down with his head on his knees, watching something move in the dirty seawater that was covering the floor of the cellar. He suddenly threw his right hand forward and snatched whatever it was from out of the water. He had been locked up in that dungy cell for close to a week by then and he was looking for something more than bread and water to put into his belly.

Like Wart had done before, Waxer had caught himself a crab creature to eat. He stood up, holding the squirmy thing in his hand. The crab creature was small and ugly, spongy and slimy. The head resembled a vampire bat with large teeth protruding out of its mouth. Its eyes were large with red and yellow eyeballs. The whole of the creature's face looked like it was nothing more than a pus-filled pimple on someone's very greasy, very ugly face.

The hideousness of the creature, as well as his hunger pains, disappeared once Waxer heard the sound of Dalina and several children coming into the large room above him. Still holding his mud-drenched meal in his fingers, Waxer quietly moved to the staircase and positioned himself under the trap door to try and get a better look.

In the spacious, two-story room above Waxer, the children stood mesmerized by a magical-looking contraption—a carousel that covered the whole of the floor space in the large open room. This was not your normal, horse-and-buggy merry-go-round; rather, the figurines were all in the shapes of flying insects—big, cute bugs.

There were flies, grasshoppers, dragonflies, beetles, locusts, bumblebees, wasps, and butterflies. They were colorful and very exotic, with many lights all around. Each of the figurines had wide, happy grins on their faces, and was built so realistically they appeared to be alive, with real hair and fuzzy bellies. Their big bug eyes moved in the direction of the children and the manner in which they beckoned their riders proved that they were definitely child-friendly.

"Okay...it's time," Dalina declared. "Pick out your favorite bug. You're going on the ride of your lives!"

Without any hesitation at all, the children scampered onto the carousel and mounted their chosen insect.

Just below the wooden slat door on the floor, Waxer was watching as the children prepared for the enticing joyride.

It all seemed even more confusing to him. If the other kids were playing games and having all kinds of fun, why was he stuck down in a wet, dirty cellar with only bread, water, and crab creatures to eat?

"What the heck is going on?" Waxer yelled to the kids above his prison cell. "You are all up there playing your butts off and I'm stuck down here with only bread and water and slimy creatures to eat! Let me out of here! Hey!" he screamed as he hit the trapdoor with the palm of his hands. "Come on! What did I do?" He couldn't come close to making any sense of what he was watching or of what was happening to him. It did give him a small amount of comfort, though, to think that Lundon might not be suffering like him.

Suddenly and from out of nowhere, a large eye popped into view just inches away from his face. Startled, Waxer screamed out and fell back down into the mucky water that covered his prison floor. It was Dalina; she'd heard his raucous and came over to stop him before any of the kids heard him.

"You're a troublemaker! I knew it from the first sight of you! Stay away from the floor and mind your own business little boy! You don't want to know what I'll do to you if you don't!"

For just as quickly as she had appeared, she walked away just as fast, throwing an old blanket down over the trapdoor covering Waxer's view.

Waxer stood there in total shock. Not only couldn't he figure why those kids where having so much fun and why he was stuck in the cellar, he could not understand what he'd done to get this woman so angry with him. Wes, he could understand, but not Dalina. She appeared nice enough on the outside.

As he picked himself up out of the water on the cellar floor, Waxer noticed he was still holding the crab creature. Without another thought, he opened his fingers and let the little bugger fall into the mucky water from whence it came. It high-tailed it to the nearest crack in the floor to hide, hoping to never again be in the same corner of the room with that kid. Wart was enough but now…two crab-eaters?

Stepping back up to the trap door, Waxer noticed a small hole in the old blanket that was covering his view of what was going on up above him. He slowly stuck his index finger up through the wide slat and into the small hole, tearing it even bigger. He could now see what the kids were doing as he sat down on the top step to watch the show.

Dalina was attending directly with her task at hand as she inspected several wood-carved insect figures lining dust-covered shelves. She placed her finger under a large wooden butterfly and lifted it, and as she brought her hand across the front of her body, the wooden butterfly came alive and flew up toward the top of the carousel. It still looked like it was made of wood, but it was alive.

Sitting on the center of the floor of the carousel was a golden crown—a queen's crown. The wooden butterfly flew to it and lightly touched one of its points, and in sequence, all the points encircling the crown lit up. In an instant, the carousel started its slow rotation and the figurines began to move upward and downward along the long poles that held each in its place on the mechanical ride, and the children's tummies instantly felt the tickle as each of them giggled out loud, and within moments, laughter flooded the room.

Waxer was still watching from his position under the slat door as the wooden butterfly returned to Dalina's outstretched finger. Waxer's anger grew at the same rate the children's laughter did. What had he done so terrible as to warrant his imprisonment in that nasty, wet, cellar? He was having a hard time understanding, but still, he watched, hoping to see if he could spot Lundon among the children.

As the ride continued to gain speed, the base beneath the crown in the center of the carousel began to move upward toward the ceiling lifting the crown on its way. As it climbed, Waxer could see that the crown was actually resting on the head of a stone statue of Queen Dalina, the jellyfish. It was encased in a huge glass tube that was rising up from the bottom, and the higher the transparent tube rose, the more of the jellyfish statue he could see, and the faster the merry-go-round would turn.

Faster and faster the machine turned, and soon it was moving with such velocity the children and the figurines became a blur and their laughter gradually turned into loud buzzing sounds—more like an army of insects than a roomful of happy, excited children.

The glass tube in the center was the only part of the machine that was not spinning. The moment the crown and statue reached their peak, two human forms, frozen in time and hanging from their wrists, came to a stop. A sting from the jellyfish statue's tentacle had paralyzed both of the humans, keeping them from escaping.

It wasn't until the glass enclosure reached the top and turned 180 degrees that the two limp bodies could be identified as Wes and Ida.

Yup, Dalina had given Wes and Ida a bonus, alright. It was an "extra" bonus of imprisonment inside her magic merry-go-round. *How perfectly delightful was that!* Waxer thought to himself.

As the carousel gained even more speed, and the buzzing sound of the children grew louder, Dalina walked up a spiral staircase that led to a second-story catwalk overlooking all the action below. She watched the spinning with great joy, and believed that this batch of kids was possibly the best she'd ever had on her ride. She raised her arms and spread them out in front of her as she raised her voice to be audible even over the ear-piercing ruckus of the children.

"Rise and come before your queen!" she commanded, now feeling all the power she possessed within herself.

One by one, oversized bugs—insects—flew out of the spinning ride. The faces on each of the bugs were clearly identifiable as the children. It was easy to see who was who, and they all had been turned into the type of flying bugs they'd chosen to ride. They were still wearing the same clothes they had on when they climbed on the carousel. Their heads and torsos looked human but from the waist down they were clearly insects only with human clothes on.

As any creature experiencing its first flight, the children were ecstatic, flying up and down, darting and diving here and there. They loved that they were actually able to fly and when they spotted one another, they laughed and screamed with glee at how they all had turned into cute bugs. This was truly something their parents never could have done for them.

Waxer couldn't believe his own eyes. The fear on his face told it all as he now knew what was in store for Lundon, and who knew...maybe him, too.

All of the insect children, like obedient soldiers, flew up into formation in front of Dalina.

"You are now ready for battle. Your mission is to destroy the human race with your arsenal of disease, as they have done down under the sea. Your target is their crops, their food supply, their air and their water. They killed my child, so I took thee! Go forth my lovelies and serve only me!

The hovering bugs watched as the ceiling opened, exposing the sky high above them. Determined to serve their queen, they squinted their eyes and charged up and out of the building. The wind around Dalina intensified into a violent rage, blowing her hair wildly as she continued her war—her revenge against the human race.

Down in the cellar, Waxer backed down from the stairway and returned to the block in the wall that he had been working on. Remembering vividly what he had just seen, he knew he had to work much harder, and way faster. He also knew that somehow, someway, he had to try and get to Lundon.

He took his shark-tooth necklace and began cutting more mortar away from the wall. It soon became evident to him that he would need a longer tool to work with. He looked around, reached over and pulled one of the larger creature skeletons closer to him. He broke one of the long tusks and started working frantically on scraping between the wall blocks. He kept a close watch on the cellar door as he worked, and hoped that Wart wouldn't drop in on him like before. He knew too well what was going to happen if he could not get out of that cellar.

Back in Florida, inside the merry-go-round building that Rolley owned and operated—on the same pier where Lundon used to play—Rolley was removing a beautifully carved horse figure from his carousel.

"Hi!" Sonia said as she quietly stepped up to where Rolley was working. "How ya doing?"

"Great!" he shouted, startled that she had walked in on him that way. "I'm about ready to put one of my own carved figures on this baby. How's everything with you?"

"I'm okay," Sonia answered as she moved closer. "But there are still a few things I need to figure out."

"You still think Lundon took the bridge down to Kevin, don't you?" Rolley asked.

"I think so, but I'm not sure anymore. That's kind of why I'm here. Could you go back down to the cliff wall and see if there is any sign of Lundon or her Popsicle-stick bridge?"

"Sonia, get real!" Rolley said, looking up from his work and staring right into her eyes.

"I can't help but think there might be some answers for me down there. Isn't that where this whole thing started? You saw it yourself."

"There is nothing darker than the ocean at night and a flashlight can play tricks on a person down there. I'm not sure *what* I saw anymore," Rolley admitted, hoping to talk her out of something so dangerous, and something that would no doubt end up being just a big waste of his time.

"No! That's what the detective wants you to think," Sonia argued. "You know darn well you saw Kevin pulled into the rock wall. Rolley, you said you would help me whenever I needed you. Come on, just one little dive. Please?"

"Sonia!" Rolley pleaded. "I lost my best friend there. The ocean terrifies me now. I can't! I'm sorry. You, more than anyone, should understand that."

"I guess I can understand that," Sonia admitted as she thought long and hard about Rolley's statements. "You think I've lost my mind, don't you?"

"Sit down!" Rolley ordered, with enough tact to comfort her, but stern enough to engage her listening powers. "You want my help? Here it is. This is the reality of it all as I see it. You ran into the ocean and one of the larger waves knocked you down. The sudden shock of not knowing where Lundon was, combined with your fear of the ocean, caused your imagination to take over. There was no jellyfish. Waves, yes...but no jellyfish! It was just your imagination getting the best of you, and that's it."

Sonia sat deep in thought, trying desperately to comprehend what was really going on with her life. She knew Rolley was right but still couldn't fathom what it all meant.

Losing her husband, well, yes, a scuba diving accident; those things happened in the real world, but losing Lundon without even one single sign or hint of what happened to her. That was just too much for Sonia to grasp let alone deal with. It didn't seem possible to her.

"It's like the little starfish or the talking dolphin Kevin and Lundon always spoke about. None of it makes sense, so, where is my little girl—my baby? When it comes right down to it, the answer to that question is the only thing on this whole earth I want to know."

Rolley and Sonia had nothing more to say as they stared at each other, thinking about what has to be next.

The only light in the spacious, four-kid bedroom was the moonlight shining through the window closest to Lundon's bed. The other three children were sound asleep in their own beds, but Lundon was too preoccupied to sleep, so she sat on her bed and gazed out into the moonlit sky through the glass panes. Lundon was thinking about everything that had happened to her since she had been taken from her home—from her life. Lundon missed her mother so much she couldn't stand it and she wondered if her mom was okay, and if her daddy and Jumper had made it home yet.

Up until that moment in time, those were the only thoughts that occupied Lundon's mind—Lundon's heart. The crazy talk about her mother not wanting her, or that she wanted Lundon to learn how to have fun. Well, that was just 'adult noise' as far as Lundon was concerned and had not meant anything to her.

As Lundon thought about her dad, though, she knew he probably hadn't made it back home yet because he would have come and saved her if he had. That she knew without a doubt.

Then a soft, quiet sound of someone entering Lundon's room made her turn her head from the window to see who it might be. For just an instant, the image of her father flickered in and out, but the moonlight was not bright enough to show him clearly.

"Pops? You did come to get me, didn't you?" Lundon whispered as she moved closer to the bottom of her bed. For one split second her heart overflowed with great happiness. She strained her now tear-soaked eyes trying to see if her daddy was there to take her home for real.

"Dad? Daddy?" she whispered with hope and anticipation, as the image tiptoed toward her bed.

The shadowed figure stepped into the moonbeams. It was only Dalina.

"Shhh!" Dalina muttered as she sat next to Lundon on her bed. "You should be sleeping," she said, wiping a lock of Lundon's silky brown hair off her face.

"I thought you were my father," Lundon sadly proclaimed, her eyes desperately begging for answers. For a short, fluttering second she was sure her dad had come to take her home.

"Oh, sweetheart! Don't you see? This is exactly why your mother sent you to me," Dalina said not missing a beat.

"Why doesn't she want me anymore?" Lundon asked, with tears streaming down her smooth cheeks. It was all starting to take its toll on her.

"Well," Dalina began to answer, "it's because of all the crazy things you believed in." Dalina emphasized the past tense of 'believe'. "But most of all, your mother wanted you to realize that your dad is in heaven, and he is never coming home. You have to forget about your old life and start having some fun in this new one."

A large smile graced Dalina's lips as she started flapping her arms. "I'll bet you never learned the butterfly's song, right?" Dalina asked as she began singing one of her favorite songs.

"Flutter - Flap - Fun...Flutter - Flap - Fun...Flutter - Flutter - Flutter - Flutter - Flutter - Flap - Fun..."

Dalina stood up and walked out of the room, still flapping her arms and singing the cute song as she moved. She blew Lundon a kiss and waved good night as she shut the door behind her.

Lundon leaned back against the bed rail, thinking about what Dalina had just said to her, and then she again focused her attention out through the window, out where her thoughts had been earlier.

"I didn't mean to be bad, Momma!" Lundon declared out loud as tears continued to flood her eyes. "I won't talk to the fish anymore, I promise. If you let me come home, I'll never talk about my father again if that's what you want!" That was all she could take as she started crying harder, wanting her mom and missing her dad. Dalina was finally winning. "I don't want to have fun; I want to be with you. Please Momma, let me come home!"

Each tear glistened against the moonlight like small liquid diamonds tumbling down her cheeks. Dalina had successfully confused her to the point she wasn't sure what was real, and what was not.

"You must be hungry!" Sonia said as she bent down to look into Lundon's fish tank. Fang, the little rejuvenated fish of Lundon's, swam up to the glass and looked right into Sonia's face.

"I forgot all about you guys being in here," Sonia said, looking around the area for something to feed them. "Let me see, what does Lundon have for you?"

After spotting a selection of fish food, she sprinkled some in the tank. Fang charged after the flakes and ate as fast as he could before the others discovered the morsels. Within seconds though, the other fish swam out from the shadows, darting aggressively at the food as though it were the last meal on earth.

Watching all of that, Sonia noticed a picture that Lundon had hand drawn on a piece of plastic and placed into the bottom of the tank. It depicted three jellyfish characters and under each character was "The King," "The Queen" and "The Princess," neatly written in Lundon's handwriting.

Next to the jellyfish was a drawing of a scuba diver and a dolphin. At the top of the thin piece of plastic, Lundon had written the words: 'To Daddy and Jumper.' As Sonia looked back at the jellyfish drawings, it hit her.

"Jellyfish? Oh no! The queen is a pink jellyfish!" Sonia yelled as she stood straight up and rushed to the window. The look in her eyes was one of total confusion, frustration and fear. *Could all of Lundon's make-believe world be real?* The thought haunted her as she slipped deeper into her thoughts.

Waxer had finally cut the block free and struggled to lift it away from the wall. The moonlight beamed into the cellar through the open hole. From the looks of it, there was now nothing standing between him and freedom. He wasn't sure how he'd be able to help Lundon though, from outside the wall. They'd been there almost two weeks by his count and he'd never seen hide-nor-hair of her since they arrived. He had thought he would try and find a policeman to help him, but hadn't thought much beyond that.

As Waxer's mind raced with excitement, he noticed a reflection of Wart staring up at him from the water on the floor. Startled, Waxer dropped the heavy block, shattering the reflection as he looked up quickly. Wart was sitting on the top step observing him. He had entered without making a sound and apparently had been watching Waxer for some time.

"What a foolish boy you are," Wart said in a deep and scary voice.

Waxer quickly headed for the hole in the wall, knowing that it was now or never for him. Not missing a beat, Wart jumped down off the steps and went after him, and by the time he reached Waxer, the surfer had wiggled his body halfway out of the hole. Grabbing both of Waxer's feet, Wart yanked him back into the cellar, holding him up at face level. The revolting looking old man was unnaturally strong. He didn't even have to strain one muscle as he held Waxer up with one arm.

"Dalina isn't going to like this!" Wart growled.

Waxer reached up with his shark's tooth necklace and ripped it hard across Wart's face. Blood shot out in every direction.

Angry and in pain, Wart threw Waxer across the cellar. Waxer landed on top of several creature skeletons piled up in the corner, crushing many of their old warped and waterlogged bones. Wart, not being able to see out of his blood-drenched eyes, ripped the staircase from the wall, and as he lifted it up, one of the exposed nails slashed into his pant leg, tearing a large hole in it, and exposing his leg. Wart was really only half human. From the waist down, he was a hairy insect—a big, ugly bug.

Wart threw the staircase, smashing it against the wall just above where Waxer was sitting. Waxer grabbed two large tusks, each connected to a skull, and jumped up to swing them hard and fast at Wart, hitting him square in the face.

The bones exploded into pieces as they smashed against Wart's jaw, knocking him unconscious. He fell hard against the wall, landing just below the cellar door. Waxer didn't waste even one second as he stepped up onto Wart's head, using it as a step, and climbed up out of the cellar. He was finally free and still inside the yard where he could try and find Lundon!

The huge butterfly-shaped door to the carousel building that looked out over the yard slowly opened as Waxer stuck his head out and looked around the night-drenched yard. He cautiously stepped out and after a moment ran across the open yard toward the main house. As he made his way over the grass and around the toys and rides, the moonlight cast a giant shadow of him that magnified his every move. He worked his way to the big white house and crept up to a window to peer into one of the rooms.

"Lundon? Lundon?" Waxer whispered, "Are you in there?"

Suddenly a head popped into view from inside the room, scaring the dickens out of him. He jumped back, away from the window. It was a 10-year-old girl from the new Butterfly Group.

"She's not in here! She has to be a Butterfly before she can stay in here," she answered in a not-so-subdued voice.

"Do you know where she is?" Waxer asked, motioning with his hands for her to answer his question in a lower voice.

"Yes, but I'm not telling you," the girl said even louder than before. "You're not supposed to be here!"

"You gotta get out of this place," Waxer warned. "They're gonna turn all of you into big bugs. Tell everyone to run for it."

"I'm going to tell on you," the girl said, yelling those words as she hurried away from the window.

Waxer realized she was hopelessly brainwashed, and under Dalina's control. He also knew he would be caught if he continued to hang around that part of the yard very long. He quickly ducked back into the bushes and was gone.

At that same time, Dalina, who was already inside her underwater tank for the night, was being briefed by three of her Royal Guards. Varkor, the captain of the Guards who had accompanied the king and his daughter the day the Mutant Monsters had grabbed them, and two of her most trusted personal bodyguards, Hank Hammerhead and Tenoch.

Tenoch and Hank Hammerhead were not only trusted bodyguards, but also important military advisors to the queen; literally two of her most loyal subjects. Tenoch was so famous in the fish kingdom that he'd become a legend and was known throughout the whole of the water-world. He was also one of the main characters in many of the stories Jumper shared with Lundon and Waxer.

Swimming directly in front of his queen, Varkor was talking on a shell-e-phone to some fish from down deep in the sea.

Shell-e-phones were the sea-world's answer to the human's cellular phone. From his conversation, it was obvious that he was getting some bad news.

"Your Highness!" Varkor said after hanging up the shell-e-phone. "We have a problem."

"A problem, Captain Varkor?" Dalina questioned.

"Jumper escaped from his cell last night and has taken Paco from the Coma Suppression Chamber."

"You WILL find them!" Dalina angrily ordered. "They are not to get anywhere near Lundon's mother. With Paco's magic they could somehow find a way to make her believe, and that will destroy my spell over Kevin O'Malley. Do you understand what that means?"

"Your will be done, Your Majesty" Varkor said as he valiantly obeyed his queen. "If they're still in the ocean, I will stop them!" Varkor promised as he and the others immediately swam out through an opening to Dalina's bedchamber.

Angry that her plan for total control over Lundon and her father was in jeopardy, Dalina sped up toward the hatched door that led to the on-land portion of her bedroom, morphing back into the human Fairy Godmother on her way up. As she did, Kevin's body again emerged from the thousands of small particles floating on the surface of the water, and just as it had every other time, his image disappeared into Dalina's body.

Miss Missy and Miss Hope, two of Dalina's helpers were just getting ready for bed after a long day of working with the children. The business of brainwashing was not an easy task. It was a hard, drawn-out, time-consuming kind of work.

Miss Missy, a young, beautiful black woman, crawled into her bed and pulled the covers up over her body. Miss Hope, a pretty white girl from the Midwest, was still sitting at her make-up table and brushing her long blond hair. Both girls had been involved with Dalina for only a few months, but they seemed to really enjoy what they were helping her do.

Waxer worked his way close to Miss Hope and Miss Missy's window, hoping he could find Lundon there. Seeing that the two adult women were getting ready for bed, he realized that Lundon would most likely not be there. He started to pull away, and as he did, Dalina stormed into the room from the hallway. Waxer stopped—no, froze—in his tracks.

"Get dressed!" Dalina ordered in a loud, cold voice, still straightening her wig. "We're converting the O'Malley child tonight. Bring her to the carousel!" Dalina said, leaving the room without another word.

Miss Hope looked at Miss Missy, who was crawling out from under her blankets. As she stood up and lifted her nightgown to change her clothes, Waxer's eyes bugged out of his head. Like Wart, Miss Missy was an insect from the waist down.

Miss Hope stood and she, too, lifted her nightgown up to put her uniform jeans on, exposing what her lower body looked like. She was part bug also, with thick, stringy insect hair, and bony, stick-thin legs.

Still freaked out, Waxer backed away from the window to gather his thoughts. Suddenly, the front door to the house flung open. Waxer ducked down, hiding himself behind a small bush, hoping that Dalina would not find him. Dalina and two male guards stormed out of the house, heading directly for the carousel building.

Waxer knew time was running out for Lundon and he wasn't certain if he could do anything to save her. The only thing he knew for sure was that he had to try, and at least he wasn't still down in that cold, wet, creepy cellar. He wanted to keep it that way, too.

LUNDON'S BRIDGE AND THE THREE KEYS

Chapter 9

Flying High

Dalina was already up on the catwalk by the time Miss Hope, Miss Missy, and Lundon came into the large, cold carousel building.

Lundon stood in the doorway looking into the room, as she rubbed her eyes, having just been roused from her tear-filled sleep. A smile inched onto her lips when she spotted the colorful carousel.

"Come on in, Miss O'Malley," Dalina urged.

"Hi, Fairy Godmother," Lundon replied, unaware of the real danger that was just a few feet away from her.

"I have a special game for us to play," Dalina said, motioning for Lundon to move closer. "Just look at all those cute little friends of mine. They want to be your friend, too. Just pick out the one you like the most and hop on. If they like you as much as I think they will, they'll start flapping their wings and maybe even take you on a ride. Remember what I have been saying about having more fun?"

Lundon examined the carousel, noticing the figurines were not the horse-and-buggy style she'd come to know from Rolley's merry-go-round back home in Florida. She hesitated and then looked up at Dalina, not sure of what she should do. "I...I... don't like bugs and don't you think I'm a little too old for a ride like this?" she declared.

"They're not real bugs, darling! Many kids your age and older have already had the rides of their lives on this. Trust me, you are not too old. Why don't you try saying hello?"

"Really...?" Lundon said, looking the carousel over more closely as she walked up to some of the figures. "Hello Beetle. Hello Grasshopper. Oh, Mrs. Butterfly, You look cool,"

After spotting the butterfly, Lundon knew right then which one she wanted to get on, and climbed on its back without any more coaxing from Dalina.

Dalina lifted the wooden butterfly from the shelf behind her and, just like before, it came alive, flying down and touching the queen's crown located in the center of the carousel. Again, all the lights went on and the insects began to move. Lundon held on tight, thinking all the while that it was all just a fun ride on a big circling carousel.

"Dalina?" Miss Missy questioned, moving closer to Dalina. "Lundon's not fully brainwashed yet. She might not serve you once she's converted."

"She either serves me," Dalina said with anger filling her eyes as she whispered, keeping Lundon from hearing her, "or I'll add her to the bones in the cellar." Dalina looked down at Lundon and a smile came to her lips. "Without Lundon, Paco and Jumper can never reunite the O'Malley family. So either way, I win!"

Lundon was still not aware of what was happening to her. She sat upon the big beautiful butterfly as its wings and its head began to move, slowly at first, and then after a few moments faster, then faster still. Now fully awake, Lundon was starting to enjoy the ride.

Waxer had made it back into the building without anyone noticing. He was crouched down behind a large beam, watching as the carousel picked up speed. He knew he would have to do something soon—before it was too late for Lundon.

The glass tube moved higher up until it reached its crest, and just as it had before, it exposed Wes and Ida, still hanging from the tentacles of the stone statue of Queen Dalina.

It wasn't until Waxer noticed Wes was looking directly at him, that he realized Wes and Ida were still alive. Wes began to struggle, trying hard to get his hand free from the paralyzing grasp of the statue's tentacle. The glass tube was so sound-tight that not a peep could be heard outside it. No one else had seen Waxer yet, and if Wes was able to get free, Waxer knew the old man would surely let everyone in the room know where he was. Waxer pulled back, hiding himself from Wes.

Wes wanted Waxer more than anything. He worked with all his might and finally pulled his arm free from the tentacle. Instantly he began pounding on the glass tube with everything he had, trying to break it, but the glass would not budge.

Waxer watched, knowing that Wes wanted him dead. He looked up at Lundon, then back at Wes, then up toward Dalina. Waxer could not hear what Wes was yelling but he could read his lips plain as day.

"Lundon!" Waxer said, trying to keep his voice down as much as possible. "Lundon!"

Lundon heard Waxer's voice but didn't know where it was coming from. Still not aware that she was in any danger, she looked around and tried to spot where he might be.

"Waxer! What are you doing? Where have you been?" Lundon quietly squealed, excited to see him.

Waxer motioned for her to be keep her voice down, and as he did, he looked up to see if Dalina had heard anything.

"Seize him!" Dalina screamed. "There, hiding behind the first pillar."

Miss Hope, Miss Missy and two men ran toward Waxer's location. He stood up and leaped onto the moving carousel, working his way toward Lundon as the ride continued to gain speed.

"You're mine now!" Dalina laughed.

Waxer finally reached Lundon and pulled her off the butterfly. He held her hand as they jumped off, landing next to the cellar door. Knowing it was now or never, Waxer quickly lowered Lundon down into the cellar.

"We have to get away!" Waxer said, struggling to dangle Lundon down far enough to drop her. "Do just what I tell you!"

"But why?" Lundon asked, still unaware of what was really happening.

"They'll turn us into big ugly bugs," Waxer explained as he held onto her wrists. "Drop down and get out through the hole in the wall."

Lundon's feet hit the cellar floor, and just as Waxer positioned himself to join her, two large, sweaty hands grabbed him hard around his throat from behind.

"Run, Lundon!" Waxer screamed as he tried to fight free. "Run and don't stop!" He could hardly get the words out, as the grasp around his throat was so tight.

Down in the cellar, still standing in the same spot, Lundon's eyes were glued on Wart. She was afraid to move, afraid he'd wake up any moment. Wart, though, was still unconscious and still in the same place that he'd fallen when Waxer and he had fought. She gasped at his ripped pant leg when she saw that the poor man was really just half human.

Lundon knew she had to get out of there. She spotted the hole, then she looked down at Wart, and the second she did, his eyes popped wide open. Lundon screamed and ran for the hole in the wall, and just as she got her body and one leg out onto the ground, a hand grabbed her other leg and started pulling her back inside.

Yelling and kicking, Lundon turned her body around to use the wall as leverage with her one free leg. When she did, she saw that the person pulling her back inside was not Wart—it was Dalina.

Within an instant, Dalina's free hand turned into a tentacle, and during the quick morphing transition, Kevin's image again tried to force its way out of her. It was obvious he was determined to free himself. His eyes were closed as he concentrated hard, but it wasn't enough, and within seconds, his image faded back into the face of Dalina.

Struggling to keep hold of Lundon, another of Dalina's tentacles positioned itself to sting her, but just as she was about to wrap her tentacle around Lundon to inject a paralyzing venom, Kevin's hand shot out from Dalina's body and grabbed onto the tentacle, giving Lundon just enough time to break free.

Lundon pulled her leg from the hole, stood up, and ran as fast as she could away from Dalina, scaled the large wall and left the Butterfly Wonderland Home of Happiness. Within a matter of seconds, she was out of sight—hiding in the foggy obscurity of a Louisiana night.

"Come back!" Dalina begged. "Fairy Godmother loves you."

As Dalina's words echoed in the misty expanse, she reached inside herself and pulled Kevin partially out of her body. Holding his face close to hers, she screamed, "You meddling fool! You've left me with no choice. Now I must destroy her!"

Cramming Kevin back inside her body, Dalina turned and faced Wart. She reached out and stung him, punishing him for losing control of Waxer in the first place. Her power was so strong that the shock threw him hard against the far wall. She was very angry and wanted to blame anybody and everybody within reach for the fact that Lundon had escaped—that she no longer had control over the child.

Back up in the carousel room above the cellar, Waxer was still being choked from behind. When he saw that Dalina was coming up out of the cellar, he looked surprised, as though all this time he thought it was Dalina who was strangling him. He struggled to turn his head and as he did, he saw for the first time that the person choking the life out of him was actually Wes, who had finally broken out of his glass prison and was finally in a position to get back at Waxer, once and for all.

"That's right, it's me boy! Now I got ya and I'm a gonna kill ya!" Wes barked. Smiling, he picked Waxer up high over his head and threw him onto the fast-spinning carousel. Wes stood there with his arms folded, proud as he could be, knowing that Waxer would soon be converted into some insect, or better yet, turned into one of those tasty crab creatures from the cellar. The very treat Wart so enjoyed.

Dalina walked up and out of the cellar and spotted Wes standing there, free from the bondage of the glass tube that she'd doomed him to.

"Now fer you, Witch Lady!" Wes declared as he turned his attention to Dalina. "Yer gonna taste a little swamp vengeance!"

Dalina paid no mind to Wes as she walked past him. He raised his arms to grab her, but within a split second, her arm morphed into a jellyfish tentacle and wrapped around Wes's neck, stinging him. Then, with a flick, she threw him onto the spinning carousel with Waxer.

Concerned only about Lundon, Dalina continued moving up to the catwalk without giving Wes or Waxer another thought. As she reached the top of the balcony, she opened a large glass cabinet, and a huge wooden wasp flew off the shelf. As soon as it became airborne, it exploded, breaking down into smaller wasps, and after a few short seconds there were hundreds of softball-sized killer wasps flying in a formation right in front of Dalina.

"Go! All of you, and bring back the body of Lundon O'Malley," Dalina screamed, and as instructed, the swarm of wasps flew up and out of the building through the open ceiling.

Down below the catwalk, the carousel was spinning at warp-speed. All of a sudden, one lone dragonfly popped out from the top. It flew up to the ceiling. Then a small crab creature was spit out and landed on the floor next to the twirling merry-go-round.

As the dragonfly spotted the crab, it dive-bombed down to attack it, just missing the cowering creature's head.

"I'm a gonna kill dat bug!" cried Wes, having been turned into a crab creature. "Boy, someday mind ya, I'm a gonna kill dat bug!"

High up near the ceiling, Waxer, the dragonfly, was laughing as he hovered by the rafters, watching Wes try to crawl for cover.

Waxer suddenly realized he was *flying*. "Hey! What is this? Wow! I can fly!" he yelled, as he zoomed left and right, high and low. "This is SO cool!"

Then, down on the floor, the trap door to the cellar opened. Wes, the crab creature, was only inches away from the door as he stopped, unsure where to turn. He knew, without question, who would be coming up out of that square hole in the floor.

Sure enough, a moment later, Wart popped up from out of the cellar and looked around to see what was going on. He was still a bit dazed from his flap with Dalina and had not yet noticed Wes frozen on the floor right in front of his eyes.

Wes knew full well that Wart was famous for eating the crab creatures. He crawled slowly and very quietly towards a crack in the floor to hide before Wart spotted him.

Waxer watched the whole scene from high up in the rafters, and saw his chance to get even with Wes. Waxer headed down, diving into full view of Wart and Wes, stopping only inches in front of Wart's face.

"Hey, crab sucker! You still hungry?" Waxer asked, pointing at the floor where Wes was still trying to find a hiding place.

Wart spotted the creature then bent down and picked Wes up by one of his little claws.

"No! No! Don't eat me, man!" Wes chattered. "I'm rotten inside. No! No! You ain't gonna like me! No! Stop!"

Wart put Wes into his shirt pocket. "Save you for later, but man, you don't look as tasty as some of 'em..."

Waxer screeched with laughter as he turned his attention to the open ceiling, and in the blink of an eye, he too, was gone—finally free from Dalina.

Had Dalina not been so immersed in losing Lundon, she might have paid attention to his conversion, and then could have controlled his every move. If, however, someone takes a ride without Dalina's overseeing the effort, it is anyone's guess how they will turn out; especially if she had not been successful in stealing their love. As it was, Waxer was free from her control. Well, as free as a dragonfly could be, that is.

Free as a bird in flight! Waxer hadn't stopped to think that he wasn't a human boy anymore. The thrill of flight must have made it all right—and anyway, he could fly away from that evil place, something he couldn't do if he were still a boy. So for now, he was content to be a dragonfly. The only thing he needed to do now was to find Lundon.

It was very dark that night in the swamp areas around the coast of New Orleans. The fog had moved in and infiltrated the air with its dense layers of moisture, blocking any amount of moonlight that might have helped illuminate Lundon's way. She had made it as far away from Dalina's as she dared to go, and rested next to a top-heavy Louisiana Oceanside tree, hidden by the thick night shroud.

Lundon tucked her knees up under her chin and wrapped her arms around her legs. She cried as she sat alone, and what scared her most was she did not have any clue of what to do next. She was afraid to leave the safety of the tree, so she started to do the only thing she knew how when she was afraid, and that was to talk to her father.

"Pops? I know I shouldn't talk to you, 'cause I promised Momma I wouldn't. But I'm scared and I think Mom doesn't want me anymore," Lundon admitted as she began to cry even harder. "Where can I go? Daddy, can I be dead with you?" Lundon laid her head down on top of her knees and sobbed like she had never done before. It devastated her to admit that her father was not alive.

Little did Lundon know that because she'd called out for Kevin, just twenty or so yards down at the water's edge, Sparkles, the starfish, had appeared and was jumping up out of the water, trying to get Lundon's attention. Oh, how Lundon needed to know that, but the night fog was too thick and Lundon's sobbing kept her from hearing Sparkles' tiny voice. She had no idea that her beloved ocean was only yards away.

After several failed attempts the little starfish sadly stopped calling out for Lundon. Suddenly and from down under the water, Sonia's muffled voice calling Kevin's named could be heard. Sparkles' eyes grew large.

"She's too far away; I can't get there fast enough!" Sparkles cried out. But, not wasting another second, she quickly submerged herself under the water and was gone, heading back down to Florida.

Sonia was standing alone at the surf. She had not been there to talk to Kevin since the time with Lundon, but now, she desperately needed to find out for herself. Sonia had to decide whether to believe or forget about believing once and for all, and asking Kevin seemed like the only way she could find out how to believe—to believe the way Kevin and Lundon believed.

"Kevin?" Sonia muttered again, holding Kevin's journal in her hand. She waited for a moment, hoping for some kind of a sign. "Kevin? Did you really send that starfish to Lundon? 'Cause if you did, send him...her...it...for me! I...I'm starting to think all those stories might, in some very crazy way, be true. There are just too many strange things that have happened since you left." Sonia stopped and waited, hoping for Sparkles to appear. "Please! I really need some answers! Kevin..." She waited even longer this time, but nothing. "I think I've met your jellyfish queen and I think she has taken our daughter. Did she? If it was the queen who took Lundon, it's all your fault! You shouldn't have been down there in the first place. That is not our world and now you've let it destroy our family—our lives!" Sonia stopped once again as she looked up into the sky, realizing it probably was all just in Lundon's imagination, after all. Angry, she looked back down at the water. "Rolley is right! What am I doing here? I should have known this was nothing but craziness. It's not real! How could it be?" Without missing a beat, Sonia threw Kevin's journal into the thrashing surf, giving up once and for all on the chance that make-believe was anything other than make-believe.

Sonia turned away from the water, and started walking back toward her house. Just as she did, Sparkles winded and out of breath, appeared from under the water. This had been the first time Sparkles had had to travel to two people at the same time, in different sections of the Gulf.

"Sonia! Sonia! Come back!" the starfish yelled, trying to get Sonia's attention. Sparkles raised her two bottom points and formed them into a "v" at her lips, trying to whistle, but the sound was drowned out by a wave crashing over her head.

Sonia couldn't hear Sparkles, as she was too far from the water by then. Sparkles, again, sadly submerged back down into the ocean and disappeared.

LUNDON'S BRIDGE AND THE THREE KEYS

Chapter 10

Friend or Foe

Lundon was still asleep under the same big tree from the night before. The fog had cleared, showing a large group of trees next to where she had spent the night. Next to the group of trees was a large stretch of beach and oceanfront, and up a ways from the shore were the massive swamplands that surrounded that part of the Louisiana coastline.

A few yards away from Lundon, in the same group of swamp trees, was a strangely dressed beachcomber. His skin was thick and leathery and his hair was jet black with streaks of gray that hung in braided locks down both sides of his face. His movements were animated and his body was stout, with a belly that wiggled and jiggled about. His big old hat and weather beaten clothes looked like a band of ageless seafaring pirates, maybe even Captain Hook himself, had recently held a 'buy one, get one free' garage sale.

The happy-go-lucky, bootless beach bum was busy preparing two fish for his breakfast and as he continued to cook, he kept glancing toward Lundon and smiling. If one didn't know any better, one would think that he was there for the sole purpose of keeping an eye on her—keeping her safe from the many dangers of the swamp. After a few more times of flipping the frying fish high into the air and catching them again with his pan, the tramp bent down and inhaled a strong whiff of his delicious morning catch. Once he had devoured enough of the scrumptious odor, a peculiar grin covered his face, and then he began to whistle a cheerful, upbeat tune, obviously hoping to wake Lundon from her sleep. Maybe it was his way of saying it was time for breakfast.

After the melody penetrated Lundon's sleepy world, she slowly opened her eyes, and just as she was about ready to greet the morning, she realized where she was, and even more importantly, she was clearly able to remember the events of the night before, blow by blow.

Lundon sat up and looked around, hoping with all her heart that she would not see Dalina anywhere. Fearing that the whistling was Dalina and her army of workers coming for her, she looked right and left, trying to find the actual direction that the music was coming from.

Off to her right, deeper in the trees, she spotted the beachcomber. The sight and sound of him cooking the breakfast and the whistling gave her an instant good feeling, especially when it became clear to her that Dalina was nowhere around.

The calm feeling Lundon had felt left as the strange man glanced her way. She instantly became afraid. Not knowing if he had spotted her or not, she stood and scurried behind one of the large trees, just in case he hadn't. For her part, she had absolutely no intention of ever trusting a stranger again.

The beachcomber had of course seen Lundon move behind the tree. He continued whistling and doing a funny little body dance while he cooked, and all the while never let on that he knew Lundon was there. He knew that she must be afraid of a stranger, and for some reason he didn't want to add to her fear in any way.

After a few moments, though, Lundon cautiously poked her head out from behind the tree just enough to see what the man was doing.

The man, still not letting on that he knew she was there, continued humming and whistling as he prepared what looked and smelled like, even from where Lundon was, a very tasty breakfast.

Lundon stood and watched until the fish were completely cooked and ready to eat. By then, the smell of the food had surrounded her, almost picking her up and carrying her off. She realized then just how hungry she was.

"Who be there?" the man asked, still not looking her way.

Lundon didn't budge.

Finally the man turned and looked directly at her, his eyes covering her every move.

"Well I'll be flogged," he squealed. "Yer a young one, fer sure!"

His voice was upbeat and happy, like a person who just saw his best friend after a long separation, and his eyes danced along with each inflection of his words.

Lundon moved a few steps back, not sure if the man was friend or foe.

Sensing she was afraid, the beachcomber gave a big happy smile, then held out his hand, and motioned for her to come over and join him. "What brings ya out here at this early hour, Princess?" he asked in a warm, playful manner.

"My legs," Lundon responded.

"Does yer dear sweet mama know where yer little ol' legs done brought ya?"

"My mother doesn't want me anymore."

"Why, I can't see any mommy not wantin' a precious little thing like you, Princess. That just can't be true!"

"But Fairy Godmother told me so," Lundon said, enjoying the fact that this warm and kind man didn't think her mother would feel that way. That was just what she needed to hear.

"Did ya hear your mama say that?" the gentle man asked, looking right into Lundon's big eyes.

"No."

"Did ya ever hear her say she loves ya?" he asked.

"Yes...all the time," Lundon answered.

"So it can't be true," he sang out as he began to prepare two plates. "Are ya hungry?"

Lundon nodded as the giggly man handed her a plate of food. Lundon wanted it, but still, she was not sure as she backed up a little, letting him know she wasn't going to trust him that easily.

"I just be leav'n it here fer ya then. If'n ya get hungry."

He returned to his fry pan, leaving Lundon free to stare at the food he'd put in front of her. He took the one he'd prepared for himself, and joyfully began to eat the meal.

"People call me Ju . . . J, Captain J. What be yer name?"

Lundon didn't answer as she studied the man's eyes. She'd been tricked too many times since she had been taken by Wes and Ida, and she wasn't sure how much she should tell this man. After all, he was still a stranger.

"Where's yer dinghy docked?" Captain J continued asking.

"Huh?" Lundon answered, not understanding what he meant.

"Where do ya hang yer hammock?"

"What?" Lundon asked, cleverly being diverted from her fears by the strange questions the sly quirky man was asking.

"I mean, where be yer port? You know, where do ya dock yer ship?"

Lundon moved a few steps closer. "My ship?"

"Yeah! Come on; help me out here, Princess! Where do ya drop yer anchor?"

"Are you tryin' to ask me where I'm from?" Lundon finally asked.

Captain J smiled and nodded his head.

"Oh!" she said, thinking the whole time that he sure talked funny, but somehow she was starting to feel a little safer. "From Clearwater, Florida."

"You mean you be charted all the way to Florida? Whoa, Princess! That be a long journey by foot," Captain J bellowed. "I could tell ya a tale or two about me and them there Florida waters, yes I could."

"Is it really far?" Lundon asked as she finally took a bite of the fish the old man had cooked for her.

"Yep! But nothin' like me trip to China."

Lundon started to feel even more comfortable with this delightful gentleman as she felt she could share more with him.

"Lundon," she said, finally answering his earlier question about what her name was.

"No! I said China, Princess. China."

"No! My name is Lundon," she responded with a slight amount of laughter in her voice. "Only spelled with a 'u' instead of an 'o'."

"Well now, that there's a royal enough name. How did ya end up marooned here, Princess Lundon?" Captain J asked.

"Someone used to call me that..." Lundon said, as a touch of sadness entered her speech.

"Someone? Someone who?"

"It doesn't matter. I think he's dead now," Lundon sadly answered.

A low-pitched, buzzing sound became audible. Captain J looked up to the tops of the trees around them. A serious look fell onto his eyes as he saw several wasps hovering overhead, looking down on him and little Lundon.

Though they were wasps, they were much bigger than normal, and since they looked like they had been carved out of wood, they looked stronger, to boot.

"Whoa! Look at the size of them pirates!" Captain J said with a flicker of warning in his voice.

Lundon looked up and saw the wasps staring down at her, then within only seconds, they were on top of her. Captain J began swatting at a few of them with his hand, but he couldn't stop them, and they were soon swarming all over and around Lundon. He reached for his gear and grabbed his fishing pole.

The moment he touched the pole it illuminated, like it was alive and had just been woken from a deep sleep. "I wish for a large flyswatter!" Captain J yelled as he held the pole up into the air, and within seconds the top part of the pole magically turned into a large flyswatter.

Lundon cried out for Captain J to help her, but by the time he was able to reach her, the wasps had already lifted her up off the sand and were starting back in the direction of Dalina's swamp-lands.

Captain J swung the large fishing pole-turned-flyswatter, knocking several wasps away. His quick movements were more like a skilled tennis player than a sword-fighting pirate, as he moved around swinging here and there, not missing once.

Finally Lundon dropped back down to the sand and after a few more failed attempts at getting at her, the wasps, battered and defeated, retreated up and away from the area.

Captain J lifted Lundon to her feet. "Come on Princess. It's time to hoist the main sail. We gotta shove off."

Lundon brushed herself off as Captain J gathered his gear, and the two dashed onto the beach, to move to another, hopefully safer, location.

Later that same day, Sonia was alone in her home, reading a booklet on missing children's agencies. A knock on the door pulled her from her concentration.

Standing at Sonia's door was Wanda, Waxer's mother, and she looked very worried about something.

"I'm very scared," Wanda said, getting right to the point of her visit.

"What's going on?" Sonia asked.

"My son! I need to let my son know how much I love him. I should have told him that before but I didn't think he wanted to hear it. How can I let him know? Is it too late? Please tell me it is not too late!"

Sonia could feel Wanda's pain as she pulled Wanda to her, holding and hugging her—the kind of hug that only mothers under their particular situations could understand.

"You will! It's not too late!" Sonia said, trying to give Wanda some encouragement. "I promise you'll get that chance. I don't know how yet, but you—no, we—will get that chance again!"

Captain J and Lundon had found a safer place to set up camp for their first night traveling together. They had walked a good distance that day, and were both tuckered to the bone.

"Gee, I'm sure hungry, Captain J," Lundon said, as Captain J started a fire. By then, Lundon felt not only comfortable with the man, but also believed that she was totally safe as long as he was around.

"Well now, I reckon a fisherman of my skills can muster up somethin' tasty to eat. I've been catchin' fish since I was fin-high to a seashell. Oh, I mean knee-high, Princess, knee-high."

Captain J took his fishing gear out of his pack and headed down to the water's edge to catch the evening meal.

As fishing poles go, Captain J's pole took the prize. The bright-colored reel was larger than a normal fishing reel and looked like something Bugs Bunny or Mickey Mouse would use to fish with. Captain J had even given it a name, but for some reason, he wouldn't use the name whenever he was around Lundon. By the way he handled it, though; Lundon could see that it was very special to him, and definitely a little magical. After all it had somehow turned into a flyswatter earlier that morning.

Lundon sat and watched as Captain J started to set up his gear. Lundon's attention was diverted to a large swamp hawk that was chasing after something flying around in the sky. Both were flying at lightning speed—up, down, left, and right.

Intrigued by the frantic insect that was flying as fast and as hard as it could to escape the clutches of the swamp hawk, Lundon wondered which one would eventually win the race, the hunter or the hunted.

They were too far away for Lundon to identify what kind of insect the large bird was trying to catch, but in an instant, the bug changed direction and darted down closer to Lundon, calling out her name as it raced by. Lundon didn't recognize the high-pitched voice, but questioned how it could possibly know her name.

Oh, no! Was it one of Dalina's bugs? she instantly thought to herself as she watched with even more intent. That thought scared her as she checked to make sure that Captain J wasn't too far away, just in case.

After a few more seconds, still afraid that maybe Dalina had something to do with what was going on with the hawk and the terrified bug, Lundon decided she'd better not take any chances. She jumped up and ran down to where Captain J was fishing.

"What's wrong, Princess?" Captain J asked, noticing she seemed afraid.

"I think more bugs are coming."

Captain J looked up into the sky to check for himself, but when he saw the swamp hawk, he relaxed.

"Nah! It's just a nasty ol' swamp hawk trying to catch its supper, too."

"Captain J? I like you," Lundon declared out of nowhere.

Captain J beamed with pride over Lundon's sweet but unexpected declaration of her feelings.

"Are you ever gonna catch anything?" Lundon asked, partly joking and partly serious. After all, she was hungry.

"You just keep that ol' fire a burnin' and leave the catchin' to me," he said, smiling his big, warm smile down at her—making her feel loved and cared for.

Lundon headed back up to the camp area.

"Did you hear that, Mate?" Captain J said as he looked down at his pole, whispering so Lundon wouldn't hear him. Seconds later and just above the reel, two large eyes opened and stared back up at Captain J.

"She said she likes me. She's a startin' to trust us. Come on, blast ya, if'n those fish don't start bitin' soon, you're gonna haveta help the Captain out with some of yer ol' fishin' magic."

"Captain?" the pole said as the area at the bottom of the handle opened up, forming a mouth with sparkly-white teeth and a big, red, sloppy tongue. "I knew I should have made you a deckhand instead of a captain!" it said.

As Lundon put some more wood on the fire, again, the same faint voice called out to her.

"Lundon! Help! Help! Lundon!"

Lundon looked around trying to identify who and where the voice was coming from. The large insect changed direction and zoomed down near her face, and a split second later, the determined swamp hawk swooped down, almost hitting her. Lundon ducked down as the smaller of the two flew down and under her raised knees, hiding from the pursuing bird.

Lundon quickly put her arms down over her legs, hiding the cute, funny looking dragonfly from the hungry old hawk.

Seeing that the human girl was very intent on sheltering its evening meal, the hawk gave up and angrily flew away.

Lundon opened her knees to take a look at what she was protecting. The exhausted dragonfly yelled up at her. "I've been looking all over for you!"

Lundon studied the noisy critter and noticed the 'Great White of Florida' t-shirt. "Waxer? Is that you?"

"'Course it's me!" Waxer said. "What other cool, slick dragonfly do you know that knows your name? Anyway, I told you the witch was going to change us into bugs. That's why I wanted you to run for it!"

Lundon reached down and picked him up by his wings.

"Hey! Watch the silks, will ya?" he shrieked.

"How did she do this?" Lundon questioned.

"She's a witch, but I gotta tell ya, I don't mind it!" Waxer said. "I always wanted to fly like the wind and now I can."

"Thanks for helping me escape. I was so scared."

"Did the witch hurt you or were you just playing the whole time like most of those bratty kids?"

"No she didn't hurt me. She lied to me about my mom, though!" Lundon answered. "We have to get back home!"

"And just how are we going to do that?" Waxer asked, but before she could answer him, Captain J's fishing pole had started jerking like a keeper had taken the bait.

Lundon placed Waxer back down under her legs. "Captain J! You did it! You caught one," Lundon hollered, showing her excitement as he tried to reel in what seemed like a whale of a catch. It almost pulled him into the water, it was so heavy.

"Whoa, Mate! Don't be foolin' around like this! Blymie! You always gotta overdo it, don't ya?" Captain J said, trying to keep his voice down as low as possible. Waxer pulled himself up onto Lundon's arm, wanting to see who she was talking to.

He watched as Captain J struggled with the catch for the longest time.

Finally, Captain J regained his balance and as he skillfully worked his line, he glanced back toward Lundon, hoping she was still watching him finally bring in the big one. But as he reeled it in, he realized it was nothing more than a water-filled, old knee-high fisherman's boot. Captain J looked back at Lundon, who was as surprised as he was—at first, but then, not being able to help herself, she started giggling about the whole thing.

"Smart aleck!" Captain J whispered to his fishing pole. He turned the boot upside down to let the water run out and two large fish fell out onto the sand. "That's more like it, Mate! But next time, cut the fake-out routine, or you'll be walkin' me plank!"

"Well next time don't use...," the fishing pole tried to finish its sentence before Captain J put his hand over its mouth and squeezed it shut, muffling its voice, "...boot bait!"

Lundon cheered and clapped her hands when she saw the two big fish flopping around on the beach. Then, Captain J, proud of his catch, tossed the rubber wader high into the air towards a large trash can partially buried in the sand, and as it started to descend, Dalina, in the form of a jellyfish, blasted out from inside the boot.

Within the blink of an eye, she began to change into her human form, landing on the sandy beach next to the surf and as she did, Kevin's transparent image again tried to pull himself free from Dalina's powers. He reached for Lundon, trying desperately to speak.

"Lunnnnnnnddddddoooooonnnn."

Kevin's voice faded out as his image disappeared back into the morphing body of Dalina.

"Pops? Pops?" Lundon cried out. "Why do you keep trying to come out of this lady's body? What is going on? Why are you in there? Is Jumper in there too? Dad? Please tell me what is going on!"

It had happened in her presence a few times now and she wondered what her daddy had to do with this lady. Why and how? Even with her vivid imagination, Lundon could not come close to figuring it out.

Dalina, now fully changed into her human form, stood on the sand between Captain J and the water. Lundon watched, scared down to the fiber of her very soul. Both she and Waxer knew too well the power Fairy Godmother possessed. Lundon was not only scared for herself and Waxer, she was horrified for Captain J, too.

Lundon ran down to Captain J, stopping next to her new protector. Waxer flew up and hovered just above their heads. To some, it might have looked as though Lundon was trying to protect Captain J, but the truth was she was so scared she needed him to be standing next to her.

"Lundon, honey!" Dalina cried out. "Fairy Godmother has missed you. Come here to me, and I'll take you back to our wonderland—to our home."

"You turned Waxer into a bug!" Lundon screamed, angry and frightened at the same time. "No! I wanna stay here with Captain J. He is gonna take me back to my mother. She didn't give me to you. My momma loves me and she always told me so. I don't believe you! Besides, you don't have a child of your own, so you don't know what a mother feels!"

"I HAD a chil...," Dalina started to shout out. Then, thinking about what Lundon had just said, she looked deep into Lundon's eyes. "Did you say *Captain J?*" Dalina questioned, accenting the J as an evil grin appeared on her face.

She looked up into Captain J's eyes. "Jumper? What is this? Are you trying to hide who you and Paco really are? Are you afraid to let her know that both her father and you failed miserably? That you, Paco and her daddy are to blame for all this? You and Paco are losers! I should have let Varkor eliminate both of you when he wanted to. You have betrayed the entirety of our world!"

Within a split second, and with no warning whatsoever, Dalina reached out her arm as it changed into a jellyfish tentacle and stung Captain J—Jumper. His body fell to the ground, shaking from the effects of her sting, and within moments he began to change back into his dolphin form. Shortly thereafter all that was left was a big wounded dolphin flapping around on the sand, too far away from the surf, and too injured to roll back into the ocean to save itself.

The thought that the J in Captain J stood for Jumper had never crossed Lundon's mind. She was stunned as she stood looking down at her father's very best friend, Jumper the dolphin. Seeing that he was dying, she ran toward him.

Dalina quickly threw her tentacle in front of Lundon, blocking her from touching the dying mammal. Lundon backed up; and remembering how Jumper had used Paco's magic during the fight with the wasps, reached down and grabbed the fishing pole with both hands.

Dalina walked toward Lundon. The smirk on her face showed that she didn't believe Lundon would know how to use Paco's powers.

Lundon, angry at what Dalina had just done to Jumper, held Paco out in front of her. She had absolutely no idea of how to make the fishing pole work, so she just copied how she'd seen Jumper do it back at the battle with the wasps.

"You stay away from me. If this is really Paco, then he won't let you get me! I'll never go back with you!"

"As long as you breathe, you are a threat to me! It's over! All humans, and especially your father, helped poison our world, killing my daughter and husband. Now I take you in order to destroy this land! The very same thing your kind is doing to my world!"

Dalina pulled back her deadly tentacle and thrust it again at Lundon. Paco instantly changed into a fire-breathing seahorse, his real form, and Lundon held on tight to his tail as his head shot up into the sky, exhaling a stream of fire to thwart Dalina's poisonous attack.

Dalina pulled back deeper into the surf, and after seeing the fierce range of Paco's magic, knew she could not fight against it, at least not right then. She dove into the sea but popped her head back up out of the water. "You've not seen the last of me, Lundon O'Malley! You'll never see your dad again! I'll see to that!" Dalina said, and in a pink flash of light, she was gone.

Lundon, still holding onto Paco, turned him around so he faced her—eye to eye.

"Paco? You are real—you are magic! Jumper's told me all about you." With the mention of Jumper, both Paco and Lundon stopped talking then turned their attention to the poor, dying dolphin.

In a blink of any eye, Paco changed back into the form of a fishing pole. His big eyes gazed up at Lundon and then he glanced down into the face of his old dolphin friend, still lying on the sand. Jumper had only enough strength left to move his tail up and down.

"I waited and waited for you," Waxer said as he moved closer to the beached dolphin, hovering over Jumper's head, staring into his eyes. "You never came back! Now what's this...you're gonna die, too?"

Waxer, tired of having to cope with this kind of loss, angrily flew off to deal with it by himself.

"No, Jumper...you can't die!" Lundon cried as she turned to Paco. "We can't let him die! Please help him!"

"Dalina's poison is too strong for any of my powers," Paco declared.

"But we have to!" Lundon again pleaded.

"I know of only one person who uses the medicine from the land and the sea. It will take both to help him now. Yep, she might be the only hope," Paco said, turning back to face Lundon. "If you believe he can be saved, then you'll have the power to wish it. Grab my nose and make a wish. It must come from deep inside your heart."

Lundon reached over and, with only two fingers and a thumb, touched Paco's big nose and pinched it ever so slightly.

"Go on!" Paco ordered. "Take hold of me like you mean it!"

"I wish..." Lundon said after grasping poor old Paco's nose so hard he could not breathe. His head swelled like a helium balloon, and all he could do was speak with the ends of his now-tiny lips. "Hurry and make your wish before I explode!"

"I wish for Jumper not to die. Please! He's got to get better... he's my friend and I really love him!"

Instantly, Paco's head and body began to change, and still in the shape of a fishing pole, he bent down and slithered, like a snake, under the sand beneath Jumper. Then, after sliding completely under the old dolphin, Paco morphed from the form of a fishing pole into a giant crocodile, with Jumper now lying comfortably on Paco's back.

Paco, the crocodile, was about twice the length of Jumper, and bore a dirty swamp-green color reaching from its nose to its tail. The only things that resembled what Paco had looked like as a fishing pole were his eyes and his buckteeth.

Paco rolled his eyes back, looking at Lundon, who still didn't have any idea why Paco had turned himself into a crocodile.

"Hop on, Princess Lundon!" Paco said after he saw that she didn't yet realize this was all the result of her wish. "There's no time to lose. This is the answer to your wish! Hurry now!"

Lundon straddled Paco, just behind his front legs but in front of Jumper's limp body. She looked up into the sky for Waxer.

"Waxer! Hurry! We've got to go now," Lundon hollered.

Waxer flew up next to Lundon, perplexed by the presence of a crocodile.

"Where we going?" he asked. "Who's this? What's going on here? Where's Paco?"

"I'm sitting on him, and we gotta go get Jumper some medicine. I think we're gonna meet Madam Lifee."

"Madam La *who?*" Waxer asked, before remembering the supposed story that Jumper never bothered telling him about.

A story that Waxer thinks Lundon just made up all by her little self. "Oh, man! Not this again! Are you nuts? Jumper's dying and you want to take him into one of your fairytales?"

"A fairytale, you say?" Paco asked, fixing both eyes directly on Waxer. "Fairytales are only fairytales to the nonbeliever!" Paco lowered his head and slithered down into the water, moving toward the deep, dark part of a Louisiana swamp.

Waxer, still not understanding the meaning of Paco's words, hovered over the land right next to the narrow river Paco had entered. He had no intention of following them into that scary, murky jungle. "I'm tellin' ya for the last time. If there really is a Madam Lifee, Jumper would have told me about her. Lundon! There's no such a place as a magical swamp! You made up the whole story!"

After a moment, though, he realized he was being left behind. He looked around and soon noticed that the area had become much too quiet. The only sounds he could hear were his own words and the heavy beating of his heart. He hovered there wondering whether he should follow Lundon when he heard a strange noise coming from high up in a tree. He glanced up only to see the same swamp hawk that had been chasing him all day looking even hungrier than before.

"Okay! Okay!" Waxer said, glancing back in the direction Paco, Lundon, and Jumper had gone. "You guys win! But there ain't no Madam Lifee."

With the swamp hawk watching his every move, Waxer took off at lightning speed, hoping to catch up to the others before the swamp hawk caught up to him.

LUNDON'S BRIDGE
AND THE THREE KEYS

Chapter 11

A Mother's Love

Sonia and Wanda were in Sonia's kitchen, drinking coffee and looking at several different photos of Waxer and Lundon. They were trying to decide which one of each to use for the missing children's fliers they planned to make and pass out around the beach areas.

Wanda, always acting the mystical one, spread Waxer's photos out over the table top. Then, natural as could be, she started chanting to the spirits for guidance in selecting the right photo of Waxer.

Sonia leaned back against the counter next to her kitchen sink and watched, suppressing her laughter, as Wanda performed her theatrics.

"Oh powers within me...Help me pick a photo of Waxer that will bring him back home to me!"

Sonia stood with her hand up to her mouth, to hide her grin, yet at the same time she felt she wanted to cry. It was funny but yet very sad, and Wanda really believed it would work, so, for Sonia at least, that one element made it all okay.

Whatever Sonia felt about how Wanda dealt with this whole psychic thing suddenly didn't matter anymore; one of Waxer's photos started to wiggle, almost as though it wanted to jump up and dance a jig. It moved here, then there, all over the top of the table.

Sonia moved closer to get a better look. She could not believe what she was seeing.

Wanda appeared to be just as surprised as Sonia. She looked up at Sonia, and then, as if trying to play along with the whole thing, pointed at that photo that was moving all over the top of the table. "I choose this photo," Wanda said as she reached down and picked it up off the table.

As she did, a very surprised cockroach scurried away, letting both Sonia and Wanda see that it really wasn't any special powers after all, but just an old house bug—a cockroach.

First Wanda, then Sonia, burst into laughter.

"The photo I've chosen of Lundon is right there," Sonia said, still laughing and pointing to the one she wanted to use. "It's the most recent picture I could find."

Wanda took the photo of Lundon and held it up to her forehead. She wanted to make sure nothing was happening inside or around the karma of that photograph.

While Wanda was inspecting Sonia's choice, Rolley stepped in through the kitchen door. He was carrying supplies to make the fliers.

"Hi. Come on in," Sonia said, her voice expressing more upbeat vibes than he had heard from her since this whole ordeal began. "You remember Wanda, Waxer's mother?"

Wanda looked up as she reached out to shake Rolley's hand. Rolley did not offer his hand back to Wanda.

"Of course I do," Rolley replied with a 'not so happy that she was there' expression on his face and in his voice. "I take it Waxer hasn't come back from surfing in the wind yet?" Rolley asked, his way of letting Wanda know that he felt she was a kook—a weirdo.

"I know what you think of me!" Wanda responded as she gave Rolley a dirty look. "I love my son! I will do anything to get him back."

"That's fine. I just hope you can keep focused on the reality of what you two need to do," Rolley said, letting both women know his point of view on the whole matter of psychic powers. "The kids were kidnapped. They didn't drown or fly away! All right?"

"He's right," Sonia said as Rolley and Wanda continued to give each other the cold shoulder. "We both have to keep our minds from wandering," Sonia added, trying to bring the mood back up a notch.

"I'm with you for now. But you have to admit there are some pretty strange things happening around this whole thing," Wanda said, looking Rolley straight in the eyes. "Keeping focused doesn't mean closing our minds to what we believe is possible," Wanda added, wanting the other two to know exactly where she was coming from.

Rolley rolled his eyes showing his disdain for Wanda and her beliefs, but for Sonia, Wanda's words hit home, and that was precisely why Rolley didn't want Wanda hanging around. He knew Sonia was fighting her own weirdness about jellyfish waves, talking starfish, and such. He didn't feel that she needed any extra help from some wacko like Wanda 'Waxer's mom' Worthington.

Lundon was still sitting on Paco, the crocodile, holding Jumper's flashlight to light their way through the dense and scary Louisiana swamp.

Waxer had caught up to them in one piece, and was sitting on top of the flashlight. He didn't believe they would actually see any Madam Lifee, or anyone who could help Jumper, but he knew he was safer there with Lundon and Paco than alone with Mr. Hawk—the dragonfly slayer.

Jumper, still in the form of a dolphin, was right behind where Lundon was sitting. With the exception of a few twitches here and there, he was motionless as Paco moved up the murky river heading deeper and deeper into the uninviting swamp. There were snakes, birds of all types, and many different animals and sounds. The deeper in they went, the more exaggerated everything became. Even the shadows seemed to be alive.

Waxer's new fan, the hawk, was following close behind the group, waiting for his chance at Waxer. It knew the farther they traveled into the belly of the bog, the better the chances of him enjoying a great dragonfly supper.

Finally, Lundon and the others arrived at a spot where a giant tree spread from one side to the other, blocking the river. There was no way around it, and there was a bright gold light shining right through the tree itself, guiding them into the darkest part of the marshland. Lundon couldn't take her eyes off the light and hoped it was the place that could save her long-lost friend, Jumper.

As they approached closer to the great tree, Corey, the gatekeeper of the magical bayou, silhouetted by the haze of the golden light, stepped out from the brightness onto a large root.

The roots, like massive legs folded under a giant, spread far and deep, and the tree itself was the largest, and the oldest of all the trees in that area of the swamp. If you looked up, you could not see the top for the clouds in the sky, and who knows how far into the ground the roots journeyed?

Corey was a tiny man who, at his tallest tiptoe stretch, would not top three feet. His clothes were woven from tree leaves and bush shreds. His smile was bright and confident. He spoke only in rhyme, and in a way that made everyone who approached the entrance to his world feel welcome.

"Who comes before me, seeking the wisdom within this tree?" Corey asked, causing Paco to stop dead in the water just in front of the entrance.

"I am Paco, the Royal Magician of the Sea. Surely you must remember me?"

"Oh yes, I didn't recognize thee. You have always been a strong ally to me, and Madam Lifee. Enter..."

"Waxer! See? It's the magic tree from Jumper's stories!" Lundon squealed.

"Yes!" Paco said as he looked back at both Lundon and Waxer. "You will not be allowed to enter unless you can pass the test. You must answer from the heart. It is there and only there that you can find the three keys. Do you believe?"

"Believe?" Lundon asked, not sure of what she was supposed to believe in.

"Yes!" Paco answered as he started moving into the bright golden light. "Believe...Do you believe in love? Do you love your mom and dad?"

"Of course I do!" Lundon answered. "And I love you and Jumper, too."

Paco's head reached the golden light beam, and passed right through it. He clearly believed. The parts of his body that had entered the light disappeared.

Lundon was next as her body moved closer to the light.

"Do you believe in 'belief' itself?" Paco's voice continued, echoing from inside the light.

"What does that mean?" Lundon asked as she reached the light but was stopped from entering it.

Paco's body continued moving into the center of the tree through the light, but Lundon was not entering. The wall of light kept pushing her back, and eventually she found herself on top of Jumper's body and was still being pushed back as Jumper's body entered into the beautiful beam of light.

Lundon and Waxer had been pushed clear to the rear, on Paco's narrow tail, and were still not allowed to enter.

"Do you believe in the impossible?" Paco's voice echoed from inside the large tree.

"Yes! Yes!" Lundon quickly answered as she was soon going to be swimming in the murky water with the snakes.

"So you still believe your father will come home, then?"

"Yes, if I can get my bridge to him," Lundon said, trying to keep from falling off Paco's tail.

With that last answer, Lundon disappeared into the brightness, and seconds later, Paco's tail passed through, leaving only Waxer hovering above the still, murky water of the swamp.

Not too happy about being left alone again, Waxer decided he'd try and get inside the tree on his own. He backed up a few feet, and then flew fast and hard into the golden glow. As unyielding as a solid iron door, Waxer bounced off it and fell into the water several feet away, dazed.

By the time Waxer came to, he found himself surrounded by frogs, snakes and other creatures, all ready for a tasty meal. He shot up into the air like a bullet, hitting the belly of the hungry swamp hawk, which was still sitting high up in a tree, waiting patiently for a chance at the dragonfly. Waxer had come up so fast that the bird didn't have enough time to really know what had hit him. By the time the predator reached out with his strong, deadly talons to finally snatch Waxer, Waxer had already ricocheted off its belly and onto a massive root of the magical tree.

Having just landed inches away from the light, Waxer spotted a knothole, like a small cave in the side of the big tree, and flew inside to hide himself while he gathered his senses. He knew he'd just come as close as he'd ever want to, to being another flying-brother's meal. After a moment or two, and feeling like he was safe enough, Waxer poked his head out of the knothole and saw the bug-slayer hovering just a few feet away, waiting for yet another chance.

Wondering if he'd be stuck in there for the rest of his life, Waxer sat down on a small chip of bark. This was the very first time since he'd been converted into a dragonfly that he'd thought of being a human again.

If I was a boy again I would show that bird a thing or two then, he thought to himself. *Even if all I could do were throw rocks at it, it would be better than being small enough to swallow in one gulp.*

He wondered, too, if he'd see Lundon, Paco or Jumper ever again. Maybe this was it for him. Even the thought of his mother entered his mind. Did she miss him? Was she alright? Was she sad that he was not around anymore? Was she relieved? Why had he been left alone in that lonely place? That thought angered him and left him confused.

"Sure!" he muttered to himself. "Just leave me here, I don't care! Everyone I love ends up leaving me. Well, I do believe in the impossible. Yeah, I do in fact believe it's impossible to love somebody who just doesn't up and die on ya," he said, now conscious that he was talking to himself.

Having been brought up around people who died or had left him, Waxer found his mind wondering through his past. He thought of his grandmother and his two uncles, and maybe even his father but he wasn't sure. His best friend Chon Min that died of leukemia, and now Kevin and Jumper....

Keeping his body well inside the hole in the tree, Waxer peeped out and saw that the hawk was still patiently waiting for him. "Hey you..." Waxer yelled. "Yeah, you, birdbrain...I love you...now drop dead!"

He no sooner got the words out of his mouth when two human eyes popped into view at the opening of the knothole. They looked like two white golf balls with a black tattoo of a circle right in the middle of each. The eyes were so big and so very close to him, that even at his speed, he felt like he was moving in slow motion as he fell over trying to get even farther back from the opening of the hole in the tree.

It was only Corey, but he had scared the stuffing out of Waxer, popping into view like that. "So there you are, my little friend from afar," Corey said as he stepped back away from the hole, disappearing out of sight.

Waxer stuck his head out to see if he could spot where the little man had gone. Corey was sitting on a large knotty tree root next to the hole.

"Wishing another creature to drop dead isn't a thing that will get you to move ahead!" Corey said as he looked up at the hungry swamp hawk and then down at the lost and lonely dragonfly.

"I know! It's just that I don't understand why you couldn't let me in," Waxer responded as he flew out a bit from the safety of his knothole. "Why do I have to play that stupid 'I believe in this' and 'I believe in that' game, anyway?" Waxer asked as he sat down next to Corey, but kept his eyes glued on the naughty bird that had, by then, flown up and was sitting on a high tree branch. "Is Jumper gonna die?"

"It depends on if you dare play. For you see it's not that you don't believe in love or in the impossible that keeps you out, it's that you don't believe in belief itself, and that's our only doubt."

"Man, you sound like my mother. Believe in belief? Doodoo Dingle was a 'true believer.' What did believin' get him? He was nothin' but a big loser."

"Ah!" Corey said. "I see that you are afraid of losing the game of the day. But you see, belief in belief itself is simply not being afraid to play."

"I'm not afraid! Well, for Jumper, maybe, but not for me!" Waxer yelled as he flew over to the golden entranceway. "Here, you want to see? Then follow me!" At that, Waxer disappeared into the light beam, and all Corey could hear after that was Waxer's voice. "Cool! Hey, that ol' swamp hawk doesn't get to believe, does he?"

Corey laughed out loud at Waxer's statement as he, too, stood up and walked into the bright golden beam of light, disappearing out of sight.

As Corey entered from outside, Waxer was hovering in midair looking around the spacious room, which was within the tree itself.

There were twisted roots spiraling into a giant staircase, circling the walls and leading up and down the interior of the tree. It was much bigger inside than it looked from out in the swamp—an entire world larger. Isolated sections of the walls encircling the interior of the tree were flowing with spring water, clean and sparkling, flowing upward, high into the tree, then it fell down to the beautiful, peaceful pool at the bottom several stories below.

Standing next to the large pool of water was an exotic black woman who was clothed only in natural fibers from the swamp. She was the one and only Madam Lifee, the keeper of the birds, the bees, the greens and the trees. She was of the water, both river and sea; and was part human, part flower and part tree.

Waxer was spellbound as he took in this magical sight. It took several minutes, but after flying down to the bottom, Waxer joined Paco with Jumper still lying on his back. Madam Lifee was standing over them with Lundon standing next to the pool, in front of Madam Lifee.

Corey moved next to Madam Lifee while Waxer flew straight down and landed on Lundon's shoulder. He could not take his eyes off Madam Lifee...one, because she was so beautifully different from anyone he'd ever seen before; and two, he knew he was going to have to get all over Jumper, once he got better, for only telling Lundon about Madam Lifee.

"He believes in all three, I see!" Madam Lifee declared after noticing Corey and Waxer.

"Oh, yesiree!" Corey answered as he winked at Waxer and Lundon.

Madam Lifee took a small stick and dipped it into a large pot of boiling solution she'd been mixing. She dropped a few drops from the tip of the prong into Jumper's eyes. Nothing seemed to happen.

"Corey? Would you bring to me a few drops of the sea?" Madam Lifee asked as she poured more dried leaves into the large pot.

Corey moved to the medicine shelves where there were hundreds of herbs, plants, liquids and all manner of things kept in old jars of every shape and every size. He took one of the jars of seawater and handed it to Madam Lifee. She held it up in front of a candle to get a look at it.

"Dead!" she cried. "Oh dead, dead sea, what's the future of Jumper to be?" With a worried expression on her face, she turned to Corey. "Oh pray, is there still some medicine from the tree?"

"Oh my, oh me," Corey explained. "There is no more medicine from our tree! It's as dead as that bottle of the sea."

"Oh land, oh sea!" Madam Lifee wailed. "How could this be? I've been given the powers of life, I am Madam Life...e! I've nurtured the greens, the blossoms and the bees. I've forged the majestic growth of all these trees, but now, oh land, oh sea... someone has poisoned thee."

"Oh, Madam Lifee," Corey exclaimed. "How can we make them see?"

Lundon wondered what all this meant. She moved closer to Paco and Jumper. When she reached them, with one lone tear rolling down her cheek, she faced Madam Lifee. "But we can't let him be dead," Lundon pleaded.

"He surely soon could be, pray without the medicine from our tree, and with this dead water from the sea." Madam Lifee declared. "The only other hope is true love from you and me!"

"Oh, Jumper! I love you," Lundon cried. "I really, really do!"

Lundon looked into the faces of everyone around her and then she looked back down at Jumper.

"Jumper!" Lundon said in an angry voice. "Pops told me you didn't like quitters. You can't quit now!"

Madam Lifee and Corey were surprised at how much this little girl did believe. Then, Jumper started to move one of his fins slightly, then his eyes tried to open; but after a moment, he stopped moving at all.

Fearing the worst, tears streamed down Lundon's face as she looked up at Madam Lifee. Noticing the tears in Lundon's eyes, Madam Lifee realized what was missing. She reached down and scooped up one of Lundon's tears with the tip of one of her pinky fingernails, like a little scoop, and then dropped it carefully onto one of Jumper's eyelids.

"This surely will do—though it is but a small part. For even a single drop of pure love can be the greatest cure, if it comes from your heart!"

Slowly but surely, Jumper's nose started to wiggle and then his eyes popped open wide.

"See, I knew you wouldn't quit!" Lundon screamed.

"I...don't...believe...it!" Waxer yelled. Then he noticed that everyone had looked at him when he said those words. He smiled and started to stutter. "No! I don't mean I don't believe! I believe, I...Well, I do believe, but what I said was just an expression. What I meant to say was 'YES!'"

Jumper began to turn back into the human form that he had

as Captain J. He sat up and smiled at Lundon and the others, thankful for what they had done for him.

Laughter covered the whole room and even Paco's crocodile smile covered his entire face as he too was glad that his old friend had been saved. This one was too close for comfort. Suddenly Paco exploded into a pillar of smoke and when it cleared, he was the same old loveable fishing pole.

LUNDON'S BRIDGE AND THE THREE KEYS

Chapter 12

Wishing for a Good Queen

Sonia, Wanda, and Rolley were busy passing out fliers of Waxer and Lundon. They walked from one end of the boardwalk to the other, not missing anyone who would take the photos and information of the kids.

The hardest thing for Sonia in the aftermath of losing Lundon was the helplessness she felt in not being able to do something—anything—to try and find her daughter. So much time had been wasted as far as she was concerned.

The passing out of fliers was, for both Wanda and Sonia, the best thing they could be doing. With each piece of paper, went a small prayer that it would be the one that led them to their children—to the true reason Wanda or Sonia even lived.

The sun was setting on the ocean over the pier while hundreds of people moved around the beach area, having totally enjoyed their day out of their homes. After Sonia finished taping the last of her fliers to a lamppost, she walked toward the stairs that led down to the sand. Stopping at the top of the stairs, she looked down at the spot where Lundon used to spend most of her time. Sonia stood there watching and listening and then looked up, focusing her eyes farther up the beach, basking in the thought of her only child. Her mood was pensive, and she was in a mindset to reminisce about those times she'd spent with her daughter. Having just spent a full day talking to hundreds of strangers about Lundon, Sonia missed her daughter more than ever. For some reason she felt extra close to her, and wanted to savor the feeling before the day turned into just another lonely night.

A few blissful moments passed and just as she was about ready to leave, she looked farther up the long stretch of sand in front of her, and noticed a small, lone figure far in the distance walking southward toward the pier. She strained her eyes to get a better look at the young person, something she'd found herself doing more since Lundon had gone missing. Instantly chills spread through her body as it looked to her like the person was in fact a girl making her way toward the pier—towards her.

"Lundon?" Sonia screamed, startling even herself. She could not believe her eyes, and was sure that Lundon was finally making her way back home.

Having said their good-byes to Madam Lifee and Corey, Lundon, Captain Jumper, in his human form, Paco, back as a fishing pole, and Waxer, the dragonfly, were walking along the beach, working their way out of the swamplands and heading toward Florida.

Waxer and Lundon were listening to Jumper tell them all about Dalina and why she was doing the evil things that she was and about what had happened to Kevin after having been sucked into the wall. He told them everything that had happened up to that moment.

They all looked rested and ready for the difficult task of getting Lundon back home. Jumper knew that all he and Paco had to do to break Dalina's hold on Kevin was to keep Lundon's love and belief safe and sound, and out of Dalina's control. As long as Dalina could not get her hands on the three keys locked deep inside Lundon's heart, Lundon and Kevin would be safe.

Of course, it wasn't only Lundon's belief in love, belief in belief itself, and belief in the impossible—the Three Keys—but Sonia had to believe, too, and that was going to be Lundon's job. They knew Lundon couldn't accomplish that unless she was home and with her mother. Kevin's salvation depended on his family; both wife and daughter and both had to believe in the Three Keys.

Dalina knew what it took, and she used the fact that without Lundon, Sonia would probably never find the reason to believe, and therefore, keeping Lundon for herself would help ensure her control over Kevin's body. Dalina knew that all she had to do was keep Sonia and Lundon apart and she'd have the power to come and go between land and sea for as long as she lived on this earth.

"Wow," Lundon cooed as Jumper finished his story. "I never realized Dalina is really Princess Pompom's mother, the good Queen of the Sea."

"Yeah, right!" Waxer declared. "That witch, a good queen? Talk about the impossible!"

"Well, Mate, let me tell ya somethin'!" Jumper added, with a bit more seriousness in his voice. "Before she lost her family, she was better than a good queen, she was the best of the best....

Losin' those ya love can do a heap of bad things to yer mind. Once, when..."

As Jumper began to tell even more about the queen, Lundon suddenly looked far down the beach, and for some reason, became very excited. She stopped in her tracks and stared at the pier in front of them. It looked just like the boardwalk next to Lundon's home in Florida. Lundon dropped her gear, and was drawn to the pier, almost in a trance.

"I never thought my house was this close!" *But it must be*, she thought, because that was her pier, and she could see her mother standing at the top of the stairs waiting for her.

"Momma!" Lundon cried out as she started running toward Sonia. "Momma!"

Jumper turned to see what Lundon was looking at, and could not understand why she was acting the way she was—why she was calling out for her mother. By then, though, Lundon was running as fast as she could. Jumper dropped his gear and tried to follow after her.

"Lundon?" he yelled. "Lundon! Where are you going?"

Waxer, who had been on Jumper's shoulder the whole time listening to the tales of Dalina, flew up, hurrying after Lundon.

"Lundon!" Waxer screamed at the top of his voice, flying high up over her head. "What are ya, crazy? Stop! I don't see nothin'! Stop! Your mother's not there! Now stop!"

Lundon did not hear Waxer or Jumper, even though they both called out for her to stop running. As far as Lundon was concerned, her mother was standing at the top of the stairs on that pier, and nothing Jumper, Waxer, or anyone else could say or do would divert her from reaching the arms of her mother.

The moment she approached the base of the stairs, Lundon stopped to take a breath before starting up—fourteen small steps were all that stood between her and pure happiness. Her eyes were wide open and locked onto the woman standing at the top of the stairs watching her. One beat, two beats and she was off again, running as fast as she could up the stairs to the top. Each step felt higher and farther way, and it felt like she was moving in ultra-slow motion.

There was even time for Lundon to wonder why her mother wasn't calling out for her, why she just stood there with her arms down at her side. The thought rushed through Lundon's mind that maybe her mother couldn't believe it was really her running up the stairs—coming home after all this time. Maybe she had grown too much or looked different somehow, or maybe Dalina was right; *maybe her mom didn't really want her*, she thought, as she continued her struggling quest up the staircase.

Jumper ran as hard as he could toward Lundon trying everything he could to get Lundon's attention but nothing would or could stop her from reaching that woman at the top of the stairs.

Still standing at the top of the stairs on the pier, Sonia was so touched by the feeling that Lundon was close by that she could hardly stop from reaching out and calling for her. It felt like Lundon was right there in front of her, like she was running up the stairs and would soon be in her arms; she just couldn't see her, that's all.

Sonia put her hands up to her mouth, trying hard to keep from screaming Lundon's name—afraid others would think she'd completely flipped her lid. Maybe she had, but she couldn't deny the power of those feelings. As a mother, she knew Lundon had to be nearby, even if only in spirit.

Lundon finally reached the woman, flying into her arms. Like an electric shock hitting her little body, time stopped dead still, and just as quickly as it had stopped, it jumped forward again at an accelerated speed, and Lundon realized that it was not Florida at all, and worse, the woman she had grabbed so tightly was not her mother. She was hugging a strange woman who just happened to be standing at the top of the stairs wondering what this little girl was doing calling her mother and squeezing her like she'd not seen her in a long, long time. Lundon pulled back, still not sure what was going on.

One thing she did know, though, her heart was not only pounding hard from the run—it was broken—shattered into a trillion, no, a zillion pieces.

Back in Clearwater, Florida and all caught up in her own feelings of missing her daughter, Sonia was still standing at the top of the stairs—her stairs—hundreds of miles away from Lundon. Finally her emotions surged and she was unable to hold it all in any longer.

"Lundon! I can feel you! Where are you?" Sonia screamed, as her body shook with pain, and tears streamed down her face. Others walked past her, not understanding or perhaps not even caring what this poor woman was going through.

Lundon stood at the top of the stairs, perplexed at what had just happened. The frightened woman Lundon had mistaken for her mother didn't waste any time leaving the scene. She didn't want anything to do with the confused little girl.

"Momma?" Lundon cried, as she frantically looked in every direction. She could feel her mother close by, but couldn't see her. "Momma? Mother?"

Jumper, out of breath, reached the stairway and stopped.

Lundon looked so pitiful standing at the top of those stairs, glancing right and left, not being able to understand the feelings of missing someone so much that you could *feel, smell* and *hear* them around you. After spotting Jumper waiting at the bottom of the stairs, Lundon, without missing a beat, ran down into his opened arms, crying her heart out.

"She was here!" Lundon sobbed uncontrollably. "Really, my mom was here! I could feel her!"

"Don't fret, me little one!" Jumper said as he held her tight in his arms. "We won! We made it out! See! Look at all the people. We'll just go to the police and you'll be in your mommy's arms soon! Aye! A captain's promise it is!"

"Uh-oh!" Waxer shouted. "Not so fast!" Waxer yelled, flying above Jumper and Lundon. He could see something coming toward the pier from far in the distance.

Jumper looked toward where Waxer was looking. There were hundreds of Dalina's wasp soldiers moving towards them. Many of the people on the beach had seen them also, as they too began to run for the shelter of their cars or buildings, trying to get safe inside and away from what they thought were more attacks of killer bees.

Suddenly the whole area erupted into chaos.

"Holy sea kelp!" Jumper yelled. "We gotta get to Paco before they do! Come on, Mates!"

Jumper, still carrying Lundon, started running back for his dropped gear and his ol' buddy Paco. They didn't have much time, and they knew it. The gear was still a good fifty yards away and Jumper knew that the wasps were faster and would beat them to the gear unless they ran as fast as they could and, of course, didn't fall down along the way.

It was a race to the finish, but Jumper and his crew made it to the gear a split second before the army of wasps. Having learned a lesson from the first battle, the wasps attacked them from every direction—encircling Jumper and Lundon.

This time there were three times as many wasps and it didn't take the battling bugs long before they were able to pull Lundon from Jumper's arms. Though she fought hard, she was no match for the sheer number of wasps holding her arms, hands, legs and feet. They carried her up in the air and then began flying high up over the water trying to make their way back to Dalina's.

Jumper, swung his arms and jumped as high as he could, trying with all his might to grab hold of Lundon again, but she was much too far up for his reach. He knew he had only one option left as he bent down over his gear and grabbed Paco.

Paco, having already seen the danger at hand, had illuminated and was ready to help Jumper in any way he could. There were just too many of the critters, even for Paco's magic.

Waxer did his best, using his speed and dragonfly instincts to fight them off, but again, the sheer numbers were too numerous for one fearless dragonfly warrior to fight.

As the insects forced Jumper and Paco down closer to the surf, Jumper could see the critters were dead serious this time. He took Paco by the tip of his fishing pole and began swinging him in circles over his head as a lasso. As his head circled Jumper, Paco opened his mouth and inhaled a large amount of air. With his cheeks puffed out like two balloons side by side, he began exhaling; causing strong gusts of wind that pushed the attacking insects back and away from his and Jumper's position. Jumper knew he had to keep the Paco wind machine going as long as he could, and as he did, he stepped backward, down into the tide. The moment his foot touched the water, the surf started to swell—climbing up his legs as though it wanted to devour him inch by inch from the bottom up.

Within moments, Dalina, in jellyfish form and from under the water, had worked her way in between Jumper and the sandy beach.

Then like a jet-propelled rocket, Dalina shot up out of the soup, and at the same time accompanied by an explosion, changed into her human form while she was still several feet up in the air. Seconds later and grinning from ear-to-ear, Dalina landed feet first in the more shallow part of the water facing Jumper.

Having to deal with Dalina's powerful skills as well as fight off the wasps, Jumper slipped farther into the swirling water, losing his grip on Paco and within seconds, and from the speed at which he'd been swung by Jumper, Paco found himself ascending high up into the air, twirling wildly out of control.

Now that Paco was out of Jumper's hands, Dalina knew the pole would be powerless on its own. She knew that any time he was not in his original form, he needed the touch of some other living thing in order to activate his powers. So, no longer worrying about Paco, Dalina dove into the water heading directly toward Jumper, and within moments, the two were locked together each knowing exactly what they had to do with the other.

Meanwhile, Paco, still fluttering high in the air, found himself only a few yards higher than Lundon and her captors. The wasps struggled with their precious cargo as they continued their flight over the swirling surf below.

Paco sucked in another blast of air, using it to propel himself toward Lundon. Flattening the sides of his reel into big round ears, he used them as wings and literally glided down and over to Lundon, wrapping himself around her body.

Not losing even one second, Paco encircled Lundon's tummy area, spinning like a Hula-Hoop. The wind-force from his spin caused many of the wasps to lose their grip on Lundon's clothes as they found themselves being sucked into the center of Paco's wind funnel, only to be spit out and tossed away from Lundon.

Still, though, there were so many of the flying bugs that they were able to keep Lundon up in the air and moving toward Dalina's Wonderland.

Feeling like she would soon be saved by Paco, Lundon looked down to where Jumper and Dalina were fighting, and it was very clear to her that it would just be a matter of time before Dalina was able to destroy Jumper once and for all with her powerful venom.

In one last-ditch effort, Jumper grabbed Dalina, still in her human form, around her throat, strangling her.

Dalina's body instantly turned into her jellyfish form and still, it took Jumper a few seconds to realize that he was choking not only a poisonous jellyfish, but also his queen.

"Now, Jumper!" Dalina bellowed. "You're going to die!"

"Paco! Paco! We have to help Jumper! Dalina's gonna kill him!" Lundon cried, while still trying to fight off her own captors.

Paco looked down at Jumper. He could see Lundon was right; something had to be done. Paco instantly stopped spinning, allowing many of the wasps back into the task of carrying Lundon away. "Hurry! Grab my nose and make a wish!" Paco yelled as the wooden wasps made one last effort to pull him from around Lundon's waist. "Hurry! And remember, it has to come from the heart!"

The wasps, multiplying in numbers by the second, started to make some headway in pulling Paco and Lundon from each other.

Lundon struggled to free one of her hands, and as she did, she reached and grabbed Paco's nose so hard that it almost popped his eyeballs out of his head.

"Jumper!" Lundon screamed as she closed her eyes and tried to concentrate. "I won't let her hurt you this time! I wish...I wish that...Fairy Godmother would be a good queen again."

With those words still echoing loud and clear around Lundon, she and Paco found themselves falling into the ocean below.

Waxer, who was still fighting with several of the wasps in the air just above the water, instantly dropped out of the sky and down into the ocean, too.

Dalina threw her tentacles for the final blow towards Jumper's head. Before her deadly stingers reached their target, though, something lifted Jumper up and out of the water, flinging him away from Dalina. Jumper, turning somersaults in midair, changed into his dolphin form and disappeared into the sea below.

It took Dalina a few seconds to realize that her adversary was no longer in front of her. Confused and disoriented, Dalina looked around but could not find Jumper anywhere. She dove under checking to see if he was below her, then seeing he wasn't, she hurried up to the surface and still in her jellyfish form, looked for Lundon, and when she couldn't see her anywhere either, she realized that some power greater than hers was at work.

What Dalina could not have possibly known at that time, was that Lundon, Waxer, Paco and Jumper had all disappeared under the power of one little girl's heartfelt wish.

Dalina's wasp soldiers were flying around in a state of confusion, too. Like Dalina, they didn't have a clue where their enemy had gone or what had just happened. Moments later, sirens were everywhere as several police cars pulled up to the small beach area to combat the swarms of killer insects.

Dalina submerged back down under the water as her wooden insect soldiers scattered in every direction heading back toward the safety of the swamps.

Chapter 13

The Truth Be Known

Lundon was sinking deeper and deeper, like there was no end to how far down into the ocean she could go. Even though she tried her best to swim up, something continued to pull her into the center of the large underwater volcano, eventually landing on the ocean floor inside the volcano.

Never in her wildest imagination had she ever thought that the ocean would or could be that deep. She assumed it would be deep, but deep to a 13-year-old is maybe 30 feet deep. After all, the deepest swimming pool to her knowledge was only 10 feet deep, so in order to handle those big humpback whales, the ocean would have to be say triple that at 30 feet. But hundreds of feet? That was not in her calculation range—not even close.

With her eyes wide open, she held her breath, afraid to let the air that she was holding in, out. Her cheeks puffed out so far it looked like she'd somehow stuffed two baseballs into her mouth.

She turned her head in both directions, trying to figure out how she could swim out of that strange and scary place. Soon she realized that she'd sunken too deep and she'd not be able to hold her breath for the time it took her to get back up to the surface. For the first time in her life, she was actually afraid she might die. Now in a panic state, Lundon looked around for someone to help her, but there was only Paco, the fishing pole, and he was breathing just fine.

He hadn't thought for a moment about Lundon needing to breathe. Still wrapped around her waist Paco looked up and noticed Lundon turning blue.

"Whoa! It's okay, Lundon!" Paco said, after it hit him that she didn't know she, too, could breathe under the water. "It's your wish, you can breathe, too," Paco said as Lundon tried her best to understand what he meant about it being her wish. "Look! Just breathe like normal."

Lundon had been holding her breath so long by then, her cheeks felt like they'd be that way for the rest of her life. Finally she let the air in her cheeks go, and Paco was right—she could breathe.

Lundon sat there stunned for the longest time, as though she thought each breath she took would flood her lungs and she would drown. Then, after several normal sets of breathing in and out, she became very excited about actually being under the water and being able to still breathe—a fantasy of hers ever since she first learned how to swim.

"Wow!" Lundon said plain as day. Breathing and talking underwater—now she could know for herself what it was like being a part of the ocean. She had no idea why she was there or how her wish had been responsible for it, but she didn't care. She was down on the bottom of the deep blue sea, and all she could think about was how cool it was.

"I can breathe and talk without gargle sounds!" Lundon declared as she pulled Paco closer and kissed him on the nose. Then she noticed that the others were not there. "Paco? Where are Jumper and Waxer? What's happened to them?"

"At least Jumper has to be part of your wish! My guess is he'll be dropping in any moment now. What is this place?" Paco asked mostly to himself as he looked around. Being over two thousand years old himself, Paco had been in almost every part of the ocean and remembered each place well. This place, however, didn't look familiar to him. He tried to figure out where they'd ended up, but it was a total mystery, even for him.

"Look, there's Waxer," Lundon said, pointing over to the far wall.

Waxer was still swinging his dragonfly arms and legs as he continued sinking. His eyes were closed and he, like Lundon had at first, had no clue where he was. As far as he knew, he was still fighting the wasps.

"Come on!" he yelled, still swinging and kicking. "Ya want some of me? You got it! Come on!" He stopped and opened his eyes. Once he saw there were no more hard-headed wooden wasps to fight, he scoped his surroundings, and for the first time, realized he was under the water—deep under the water.

"Hey! What the heck's goin' on here? Where are we?" Waxer asked as he started swimming toward Lundon and Paco. "How did we get down here?"

Off a small distance away, another voice could be heard. It was a very bewildered Jumper. Surrounded by a cluster of bubbles, Jumper tumbled down a long, steep embankment, heading for a very strange object at the bottom.

The object turned out to be a gigantic skeleton of some prehistoric sea creature, and it was positioned at the center of the underwater volcano. It took up more than half of the floor space of the crater.

Reaching the end of his downward journey, Jumper landed butt-first on the long and pointy nose horn of the skeleton. Feeling the sharp jab, Jumper sprang forward as he slid across the ocean floor with his fins wrapped under his backside.

Waxer headed towards Jumper, swimming circles around him as Jumper bounced across the ocean floor.

"Jumper! We showed 'em didn't we?" Waxer proudly declared.

Jumper glided to a stop just a few feet away from where Lundon and Paco were witnessing his less-than-smooth entrance.

"Whoa! That was close. She almost did me in that time," Jumper declared, happy that Dalina hadn't succeeded in annihilating him, one, and two; delighted that his friends were safe and all together again.

Paco moved closer to Jumper's face, studying it closely.

"Ay, chihuahua! Your face! Paco declared as he shook his head. "I knew there'd be some side effects if we stayed on land too long, but this...?"

"What? What face?" Jumper asked as he looked at everyone staring at him with their mouths smilingly wide open. "What's so funny?"

"You still have part of your captain's face on," Lundon said as she gave him a big hug and a kiss on his cheek.

While enjoying the attention from Lundon, Jumper noticed where they were.

"All right, Mates, what's goin' on here?" Jumper asked, moving away and studying the place over.

"I think it has something to do with Lundon's wish," Paco declared.

"I couldn't let her hurt you again," Lundon said, trying to defend her choice of wishes that had landed them all at the bottom of the ocean.

"Can you believe it?" Paco said. "Out of all the wishes our little sweetheart could have made...I mean she could have wished to go home, to be safe in her mother's arms, but no...the kid wishes for Dalina to be a good queen again."

"But this is so cool! Good job, O'Malley!" Waxer added as he spun around in delight. Then he stopped and did a double take. "Look! There's something moving inside that!" He pointed at the giant skeleton.

Everyone stopped talking and looked in that direction. Jumper began swimming toward the wide-opened mouth of the bone structure, as the others followed. A few moments later two eyes appeared from deep inside the belly section of the skeleton. Being very cautious, it made its way out from the dark section into the light, but stopped just inside the skull, not daring to come any closer. It was a beautiful little jellyfish girl.

Jumper stopped cold in his tracks. Even Paco froze, not moving any part of his fishing-pole shaped body at all. Lundon and Waxer, though, continued swimming up to the large opened mouth of the skeleton. Jumper moved forward and bowed low to the little jellyfish.

"Princess Pompom, Your Highness," Jumper humbly said, as though he were looking at a ghost. "Thank the Holy One, you are alive!"

"Who are you?" the slightly frightened, timid voice asked. "I've not seen any of you before. What does Captain Varkor want now?"

"Varkor?" Jumper bellowed. "What does that scaly, slime-suckin', belly-crawlin', back-stabbin' devil have to do with this—with you?"

"Well it is clear you were not sent here by him. In answer to your question, kind sir, it was he who imprisoned father and me in this very unpleasant place."

"Imprisoned?" Jumper asked as he looked the large skeleton over. "So that's the yellow-bellied, snail-brained, limp-finned, bottom-feeder's plan, is it? Your father, you say?"

"Varkor told the whole kingdom that you and the king had been eaten by the mutant plants. Everyone thinks you are dead! The queen has declared war on the humans because of that," Paco shared.

"Heavens, no! There is most certainly no truth in any of that," the princess exclaimed, shocked to hear such things.

"Gee! Princess Pompom, Jumper has told me all about you!" Lundon said, moving around from behind Jumper and curtsying. "I'm Miss Lundon O'Malley. I always wanted to meet you and when we heard that you had died, I was really sad; but hey, look at ya, you're alive!"

"You're the lovely Lundon O'Malley?" Pompom asked in an upbeat tone. "Jumper always speaks of you. Where is he, anyway? I miss him and Paco so!"

Lundon giggled and pointed to the dolphin with the long stringy hair and the face of the human Captain J.

"Oh my! Jumper?" asked the princess. "What on earth happened to your face?"

"What on *land* is more like it," Paco joked.

"Oh, I see. Another one of Jumper's wonderful adventures," Pompom said, smiling as though she knew about all the journeys Jumper had been on. "And you, kind sir, a friend from land I presume?" Pompom asked, looking directly at Paco.

"I'm Paco, Your Highness!" Paco declared, surprised that she had to ask who he was.

"Paco! A fishing pole?" she asked. "You certainly aren't going to make many friends down here. Not in that disguise."

Paco looked at his tail, and then wiggled it. "Oh, my goodness!" Paco screeched as he realized that he was still in the form of a fishing pole and with all the excitement of finding Princess Pompom, he hadn't turned himself back into his original form.

At that, Paco changed himself back into a fire-breathing seahorse. He, being thousands of years old, was huge—almost the same size as Lundon. He had a prehistoric look to his overall build, but still very cute and likable.

Waxer, surprisingly quiet, could not take his eyes off the beauty and majesty of Princess Pompom. He now realized that all of Jumper's stories were definitely, undeniably, and emphatically true. "Wow! You are real...ly...not dead!" Waxer declared as he moved closer toward the princess, closer to the large mouth of the skeleton.

"No! Stop!" Princess Pompom warned. "Stay back!"

Just as Waxer reached the mouth of the skeleton, razor-sharp teeth shot up from the bottom and down from the top of the jaw, making the entrance impossible for most fish to enter or exit.

"Waxer! Watch out, for cryin' out loud!" Lundon yelled from behind him.

Now it was very clear to all why Pompom had called it a prison. Luckily though, Waxer's speed and size allowed him to dodge the deadly prongs. He was small enough to move in between the teeth. He seized the moment, and took this as an opportunity to show off for Princess Pompom. As a dragonfly, he was fast and cool, and he knew it. Even down in the water.

Still, Lundon and the others were shocked at how fast the teeth closed the entrance to the prison just by something or someone getting too close and how they opened back up once the intruder backed away. Those teeth were deadly and worked perfectly to keep wanted guests in, and unwanted sojourners out.

Feeling unafraid, Waxer moved up close to Princess Pompom and with a bit of over-acting as the hero, he said: "Don't worry, Princess Babe! We'll bust you out of this joint."

"Do you really think it is possible?" Princess Pompom asked, growing hopeful that Waxer might be right.

"You bet!" Waxer answered. "If I've only learned one thing, it is that *anything's* possible." Waxer stopped and listened to himself for a moment, then, remembering there was more to his newfound knowledge, continued. "Oh yeah," he said, glancing at Jumper and Lundon. "Ya have ta believe, too!"

Jumper, Lundon, and Paco were pleased with Waxer's honest testimony of his belief. It had only been a few hours ago that nothing was possible, according to the renowned Great White of Florida, the one and only, Mr. Warner Waxer Worthington.

From deep inside the remoteness of the skeleton, the sound of someone or something clearing its throat could be heard. "Jumper! Paco! What is all this talk about us being dead and what has become of the queen?" King Pom bellowed, as he swam out to join the others. "Has Varkor totally destroyed her and my kingdom yet?"

"Your Majesty!" Jumper responded as he again bowed low toward the ocean floor, greeting his king and his long-lost friend. Still in his bowed position, Jumper's fin slowly reached over and patted the awestruck Lundon on her backside so she'd bow, too.

Quickly realizing that all the others, even Waxer, had already bowed, Lundon curtsied, holding the position until she saw the others straighten up.

"The queen and the kingdom are in great danger," Jumper said, lifting his head. "The Royal Family must be reunited before Varkor can be stopped. I don't think there is much time left," Jumper reported as he glanced at the far wall and noticed a large boulder resting up on a ledge. "Lundon, Waxer! Come!"

Jumper's mind was already at work.

Lundon was more than ready to do whatever she had to, to save her old friends and her new ones, too. She swam to the ledge as Waxer, again not thinking, darted from inside the mouth of the prison, causing the skeleton's teeth to slam closed then open again, this time almost getting him. Still acting macho and unafraid, he sped to join Jumper and Lundon.

After the three struggled a bit with the huge rock, it started to move and was soon tumbling down the steep incline of the volcano's wall.

Princess Pompom and the king moved back away from the mouth, and seconds later the boulder crashed through the opened jaw. As it did, the razor-sharp teeth slammed into the unyielding shell of the hard rock, causing the teeth to explode into hundreds of pieces. Like a toothless old man, the hole in the skeleton's head was now more than wide enough to safely swim through.

Just as the debris cleared from the shattered teeth, the bones of the skeleton began to shake. The floor under the skeleton began to shift and the walls of the volcano began to break and fall inward. The crash had triggered an earthquake...or maybe it had been rigged that way by Varkor; no one there was too sure!

Jumper, Lundon, Waxer and Paco hurried down toward the broken skeleton. Jumper helped King Pom out of the mouth and onto his back for a quick ride out of the crumbling underwater prison.

A piece of bone from the skull broke loose and crashed down, pinning several of Princess Pompom's tentacles to the seafloor. Paco and Waxer struggled, trying to help move the debris off Princess Pompom. Lundon, like a true heroine, quickly joined them; taking the bone with both hands and lifting the weight off, freeing her newly discovered sister of the sea.

Waxer took Princess Pompom by the back of her pretty pink neck and pulled her up, taking her away from the crumbling skeleton and to the top of the large volcano—the only exit out of that underwater tomb.

Lundon, still holding the heavy bone, let it fall as Paco moved to her, allowing her to climb onto his back. To her, it felt as natural as riding on the ponies on Rolley's merry-go-round back home on the boardwalk. The only difference was this seahorse could breathe fire and fight off monsters for her. Holding onto a braided sea kelp bridle that was attached to Paco's neck, Lundon prepared herself for the jaunt out of the almost totally collapsed volcano. Paco leaned his head forward, lifted his spiny tail and sped off to try and join the others in their attempt to escape in sufficient time.

They knew by the sound and intensity of the rumbling and shaking around them that the whole volcano was about to blow its top. They also understood that if they didn't make it out before it blew, they'd be buried alive.

The opening of the volcano stuck up out of the water about 20 or 30 feet. It was a tiny island with a massive opening smack in the middle of it. From the look of the white droppings all over the rock walls and outside surface of the volcano, birds were the only inhabitants of that very small and isolated island. The landmass above the waterline wasn't more than 5000 square feet, maximum. It was obviously formed as a result of the volcano.

Suddenly, the exterior floor of the volcano began to crack, and within a moment or two, Jumper, with King Pom still holding onto his dorsal fin like a rodeo cowboy strapped to a Brahma bull, shot up and out of the opening.

"Atta boy, Jumper," bellowed the king. "Let's go get 'em!" The long fall into the black, cold water below took both Jumper's and the king's breath away as they disappeared into the filthy dark toxic waters of the decayed sea that surrounded the entire circumference of the volcano.

Seconds later, Waxer flew up and out of the volcano opening, still holding onto Princess Pompom with all his dragonfly legs. Princess Pompom watched as the cone they'd just come out of cracked and crumbled beneath them, leaving nothing remaining of the volcano below. After a few more seconds, the only things in sight were large bubbles and pieces of large bones from the skeleton prison popping out of the water floating on the crests of the rolling waves. Everything else sank and was gone from Waxer's and Pompom's view.

"Waxer!" Pompom cried as she and Waxer started to lose altitude and was quickly plunging toward the water. "Lundon and Paco are still inside the volcano!"

Waxer tried to stop their descent into the open sea below, but with Princess Pompom's weight and his wings being so small, he was pulled under the water with her. Right up until they dropped into the drink, the expression on Waxer's face showed his terror and strain as he tried with all his power to keep them airborne. He was committed to helping Princess Pompom, but he also needed to be there for Lundon, too, and he didn't know how he could save both of them.

After Pompom and Waxer disappeared under the surface, there was no sign that a volcano had ever existed except for the bubbles squeezing up through the brine, only to disappear in thin air with several slight poof-poof-poof sounds adding some off-beat rhythms to the sound of the rolling waves.

Within minutes, all the rumbling and shaking stopped, and the sea around where the volcano once pierced through it like a tiny pimple on the belly of a large elephant, was gone. Then, with one last hurrah, rocks and flames exploded out of the water as Paco, using his powerful fire-spewing breath, blew one final cavity for him and Lundon as they came flying high up out of their would-be graves below. Lundon was holding on for dear life and within seconds, the two disappeared into the same section of dark black water the others had.

As Lundon and Paco slipped deeper under the water, they were met by Jumper, King Pom, Waxer and Princess Pom-pom, all choking and holding their noses. The volcano had been surrounded by part of the Decayed Sea, a perfect place to hide a secret prison from the rest of the inhabitants of the ocean. It was so polluted and toxic that nothing could live in it for any period of time, except of course, the plants that had turned into mutant monsters.

As the bubbles quickly disappeared from the crumbling rocks of the volcano King Pom looked around, shaking his head.

"The Decayed Sea! No wonder no one came looking for us," he sadly noted as he continued to blink his eyes to keep them from stinging.

"Only Varkor could have planned it this way," Jumper spurted out. "We'll all choke to death or be eaten by the mutant plants. With the volcano crumbling down, they'll most likely be coming to see what all this commotion was."

Jumper hardly got the words out of his mouth when right next to where they were swimming; several large mutant plants appeared moving closer to where the voices were. The sound and smell of fresh meat was music to their ears and meant fresh meat for breakfast. Though they looked similar to the plants that were growing in Kevin's lab, they were much, much, much larger. Some of the plants towered over 15 feet tall.

Though they had no visible ears, it was obvious that they could hear, and once they got close enough to see the new visitors, they knew a tasty meal when they saw one—and this was a six-course buffet.

Even the younger, smaller plants were twice Lundon's height and their long, greasy branches were six to eight feet long. Not wanting to waste another moment in pouncing on their dinner, the plants started advancing toward their prey much like the plants had done that morning in Kevin's lab on *Sea Wonders Research One*. The only difference was these plants were not chasing after old, rotten canned tuna; they were after Lundon O'Malley and her friends.

Waxer instinctively darted up and punched one of the plants in the eye. The mutant covered its face with its oily branches and screeched out in a loud, ear-piercing cry that echoed everywhere, summoning all the plants around them. There were countless plants thrashing up through the mud from the sea floor as they moved, all at different speeds, toward the foreigners.

Seeing that he had made a big mistake in trying to take on the hungry bottom-dweller, Waxer darted back to the others, who were already looking for the fastest route out of the toxic muck.

There were rusted, out-of-use oilrigs, garbage of all sorts, and large pipes that were secreting poison chemicals, drop by drop. There were fish skeletons that covered the entire ocean floor in that area. The ear-piercing cries were now coming from every direction, and the commotion from one, like dominoes, signaled all the plants in that area of the Decayed Sea. They were everywhere as they transcended the murky sand of the ocean floor quickly approaching the appetizing visitors.

Oil dripped off every part of their grotesque bodies. Their mouths were full of sharp, jagged teeth and emitted a roar loud enough to be heard hundreds of yards in any direction. The noise became so electrifying that oil drops, shaken off the plants and floating in the water, ignited into flames and burned up in the water. It looked like fireflies flashing inside the inky ocean waters.

King Pom motioned for the others to follow him and Jumper. They all began swimming as fast as they could, hoping to find a clear, clean part of the ocean—a place that their pursuers could not survive in.

Deep in the ocean, not too far away from the Decayed Sea, was the royal palace where Queen Dalina had lived with her husband and daughter. Now in her jellyfish form, Dalina had returned to her castle to head up the search for Lundon, Waxer, Jumper and Paco.

Only seconds passed after the queen had entered her chambers that Captain Varkor and his two bodyguards, Hank Hammerhead and Tenoch, approached her.

Hank Hammerhead's skin color was bright red and green, stripes of valor from all the battles he'd fought for his underwater kingdom. He was a good fish and was always there for the royal family in their times of need.

Tenoch was larger than Hank, but not by much. He still carried his Aztec spear and shield that he'd brought with him the day he was changed into a giant squid, and his Aztec war paint on his face remained a permanent skin pigmentation, a proof of his human past. He was the most loyal of all the king's guards. He and Hank Hammerhead had served the kingdom of the sea for more than 400 years, and had done so proudly and honorably. They were more loyal to the queen than they were loyal to Captain Varkor, and it showed.

"Captain Varkor!" Dalina said as the three approached her. "I should have listened to you when you wanted me to kill Jumper and Paco!" she said, turning to Tenoch. "I spared their lives only out of respect for the long service you've given to our kingdom, but hear me now; I will allow Captain Varkor his will once we've recaptured them."

"Your Majesty, please...," Tenoch started to plead.

"Silence!" Varkor ordered, turning to the two warriors. "You continue to make too many mistakes in your judgments lately! I will deal with both of you after this mission is complete. Meanwhile, stay out of my way!"

"Enough!" Dalina ordered, talking directly to Captain Varkor. "We can't rest until Lundon O'Malley is back under my control. I think she is here in the ocean, but just in case, I must return to land and deal with Momma O'Malley. I will return shortly, and when I do, you better have Jumper, Paco, and that child in custody, or you will see the splendor of this ocean no more!"

Varkor held his tongue, but it was obvious he held great contempt for Dalina, when he only slightly bowed his head as she was readying herself to leave.

Tenoch and Hank Hammerhead, on the other hand, lowered their heads almost to the floor, showing the queen that they respected her orders and would serve her loyally to the end.

Dalina raised her tentacles and began swirling in a tornado-fast turn until the water and bubbles totally concealed her spinning body, and then within a blink she disappeared.

Still inside the Decayed Sea, Jumper, King Pom and the others darted here and there, desperately trying to find their way to clean water, while having to evade the deadly grasp of the monster plants at each and every turn. The plants continued to pop up in every direction.

A smaller one, harder to see and much faster than the larger undergrowth, got close enough to make its move at Lundon, shooting its tongue forward, like a frog catching a fly, and grabbed onto Lundon's leg, pulling her off Paco's back.

Fighting with all her might, Lundon tried to free her leg as the small monster plant dragged her closer and closer to its mouth, full of razor-sharp and oil-drenched teeth.

Just moments before Lundon reached the grinding teeth of the monster, Paco rushed up to its elongated tongue, and with the jagged edges of his tail, like a hacksaw, sawed through it, sending the plant into a screaming tizzy fit.

Paco then hurried down toward Lundon, who was now unwrapping her foot from the slimy, greasy severed tongue, and helped her onto his back as they again sped off to catch up with the others.

Waxer, ever playing the hero, distracted several of the plants from getting Princess Pompom. He ran interference as the little Jellyfish princess scurried away from any danger. At one point, Waxer swam up and into the mouths of several plants one at a time, flitting back out just as they slammed their slobbery jaws shut. They went crazy trying to get their teeth into him. He even led one into the other and laughed as they both took large bites out of each other's heads.

Just before poor old King Pom was about to choke to death, Jumper spotted the sparkling glow of clean ocean water not too far off in a distance.

Within moments, they were all swimming in that direction as fast as they could, with the mutant plants only inches behind them, doing everything they could to keep their quarry from escaping.

Like scared rabbits running from a pack of hungry wolves, Jumper, King Pom, Waxer, Princess Pompom, Paco and Lundon burst into the breathable ocean water, coughing and choking from the poison muck of the Decayed Sea.

The mutant plants stopped just inside their border, bellowing their unhappiness for not succeeding in catching their prey. They knew they would not last even a short time in the clean water, and reluctantly disappeared farther back into the darkness of their decaying world.

Chapter 14

The Families

Rolley was working late; tightening the last nut on the grasshopper figure he had carved to replace the horse on his merry-go-round. He wiped the grease off his hands as he stepped back to admire his handiwork. He pushed up the sleeve of his shirt, revealing that his arms were textured like that of a grasshopper, the same as the figurine he was admiring.

"You've served me well," said Dalina, startling Rolley as she entered his workroom. "Is Sonia O'Malley ready?"

"Yes! I will do it tonight," Rolley said as the expression on his face changed from reflective to cheerful.

"Very well!" Dalina said, happy to hear that her plan was still on track, at least the part dealing with Lundon's mother. "From tomorrow you shall take command of my insect army here on land. You will lead them in the destruction of this environment as the humans have done to my world."

"As you command, my queen!" Rolley answered, without a hint of remorse or regret.

"Make sure she believes Lundon is dead. Otherwise, the conversion might fail."

"I have the very thing that will convince her," Rolley said with total confidence in his voice.

Dalina studied his eyes; smiled, then turned and walked out of the room, heading back down to the sea to finish dealing with Lundon, Jumper and Paco.

Jumper and the others were still coughing the vile water out of their systems and as they were able to slowly catch their breaths, they rubbed and shook the greasy muck off their bodies and out of their eyes and ears. King Pom blinked his eyes several more times and soon he could see clearly again. He and Jumper studied the area to figure out where they were and where they needed to go—getting their bearings, so to speak.

"Your Highness! I think I recognize this area!" Jumper said. "I do believe this is Seven Reefs! We should be very close to the royal castle."

"Yes, I think you're correct! Yes, indeed. I recognize it now. Goodness me! The Decayed Sea is closing in on us faster than I thought," responded the King.

"Seven Reefs?" Waxer asked.

"Each village in our kingdom gets its name based on the distance it is from the Royal Palace. We measure distance down here by reefs. This village is only seven reefs from our home. Therefore we call the area Seven Reefs because of the distance," Pompom answered.

"How close is that?" Lundon asked.

"When we were taken, I believe the black wall of the Decayed Sea was around twelve reefs. Now it has grown all the way to seven! So many communities lost!" said Paco, shaking his head in disgust and worry.

"When I was a young flapper, I used to play all over this area. There are some hidden caves somewhere around here," Jumper said.

"Look, Varkor's soldiers!" whispered Pompom, glancing toward the far end of the reef.

King Pom and the others refocused their attention on the small fish community located a short distance from them, and as expected, Varkor's soldiers were everywhere.

"Follow me!" Jumper whispered as he ducked down behind a large rock. "We've got to hide ourselves," he said, motioning for the others to keep low.

Not long after they've swam a short distance, they arrived in front of a giant shell cave situated along a tall incline where the splendor of the Royal Castle could be seen far in the distance. It was one of the most beautiful sights Lundon had ever witnessed in her life.

Captain Varkor, Hank Hammerhead, Tenoch and several of the royal soldiers were searching the area around Seven Reefs, and were getting closer to the cave area to which Jumper and the others were en route.

At that very moment, Captain Varkor caught something out of the corner of his eye. He looked in front of his troops, holding up a long seashell spyglass studying the area all around, and then he saw what he was hoping for.

"Perfect!" Captain Varkor mumbled to himself as he watched Jumper struggling to squeeze the bottom half of his body through the small opening of the shell cave.

Jumper was the last of the group to enter and Captain Varkor continued to watch as Jumper disappeared through the opening.

"Wherever that stupid, overrated, phony scientist dolphin is, Paco and Lundon will surely be!" Varkor said with a loud burst of laughter.

"Captain? I take it you've spotted Jumper?" Tenoch asked.

"Gather my army and follow me!" Varkor ordered. "Oh, yes! Summon Her Majesty! She'll not want to miss this!"

What Varkor did not know, was the only thing on this earth that could spoil his plans and expose his true self to the queen, would be the king and her daughter, Princess Pompom, suddenly showing up. That thought was the furthest thing from Captain Varkor's mind. In fact, he never intended to set his eyes on King Pom or his daughter ever again. As far as he knew, they were locked away inside that volcano and therefore did not exist.

Hank Hammerhead and Tenoch headed off to gather the rest of Captain Varkor's fish army and of course, to notify the queen.

Rolley led Sonia in through the opened door and up to his merry-go-round. It was early morning and the whole area was dark and quiet where every sound could be heard more clearly than when masses of people were scurrying around interrupting the silence. Sonia couldn't remember ever being on that boardwalk that early in the morning. It was so different—so quiet in a very forlorn way.

"Okay! Okay!" Sonia said. "Let's see what is so important that it couldn't wait until morning."

Sonia, who had been woken from her sleep, followed Rolley to the merry-go-round. He moved up onto the platform and down into the center as Sonia stepped onto the ride, stopping in front of the new insect figurine. "This is a strange choice for a ride like this, don't you think?" Sonia proclaimed as she touched the beautifully crafted grasshopper. "Please tell me this isn't what you wanted to show me."

"I found this out by the dumpster just a few hours ago," Rolley said, as he handed her a dirty old brown shopping bag.

Sonia was not sure if she wanted to see what was in the bag, or not. "What is it?" she asked opening it. She pulled out a t-shirt covered in dried blood. She immediately recognized the shirt as one of Lundon's. She dropped it and watched it fall to the floor. "No! Oh, no!" Sonia cried out as she collapsed to the floor of the carousel.

Never in a million years could Sonia have thought Rolley would ever handle something like that in such a cold, uncaring manner. Tired and totally unprepared for what she had just seen, Sonia was out cold, which of course was exactly what Rolley had counted on.

Rolley's heart pounded and his eyes sparkled with anticipation as he moved to her limp body, picking her up and setting her on the insect figure. After strapping Sonia securely on the ride, Rolley moved to the on/off switch of the carousel and flipped it on. The gears of his merry-go-round noisily screeched and groaned as the heavy machine began to turn. Sonia's limp body, harnessed to the new wooden figurine, obediently followed its every move.

Gathered in front of the shell cave, Captain Varkor's fish-soldiers had surrounded the whole area. The finned military force was quiet as they positioned themselves for battle. After a moment, Varkor moved to the front of his military force and took his place at its head, and directly behind his position stood Hank Hammerhead and Tenoch.

Queen Dalina and a large group of royal eels, turtles and stingrays, a regal caravan if you will, pulled up to the gathering.

Dalina sat on a throne made of seashells and jewels, parading her royal status there in the kingdom of the fish, as a large section of the finned-soldiers moved aside, allowing Her Majesty to join Varkor at the front of the formation.

Following close behind Her Majesty were several more chamber servants riding on an eel bus, and once the queen's caravan stopped, her servants swam off the eel and followed behind the queen as she methodically made her way to the front of the army she commanded.

"Well, Captain Varkor? This gathering better not end up being a bunch of nothing!" Dalina warned in a low voice that only Varkor, Hank Hammerhead and Tenoch could hear.

"Your Majesty! Wait until you see what I have cornered inside that shell cave just for Your Majesty's own pleasure!" Varkor said, still smirking as he turned his attention to the front of the cave.

"Jumper! It's over!" Varkor yelled, his voice echoing everywhere. "We know you're in there. You, Paco and the human girl come out NOW!"

After a long moment of silence, Jumper's voice bellowed out from inside the cave. "You are correct! We are *all* here! You must know though, we will surrender only to the queen!"

Varkor wondered why they wanted to surrender only to Dalina. He knew that in the present state the queen was in, she would deal with them far more harshly and quicker than he would. Of course, he had no way of knowing that his two, very special and very secret prisoners, were actually inside the cave with Jumper. He looked at Dalina.

"I am here...!" Dalina yelled out, motioning for Varkor to back off and allow her to speak. "Jumper? Paco? You are traitors to the Kingdom of the Sea," she bellowed, throwing her words directly into the hallowed opening of the shell cave. "With all your empty promises about this new fish you and Kevin O'Malley supposedly created that was going to destroy the Decayed Sea. I waited, and waited for you to bring me proof...but only empty words reached me!

Jumper's mind quickly jumped back to that night he'd tried so hard to get the Muck Munchers to the queen so she'd see his and Kevin's long awaited promises were actually real and could solve all the problems regarding the muck in their ocean. How he'd arrived at the doors of the queen's residence that night only to be met by the guards that had been placed outside her door. How the unlucky dolphins that Kevin had sent to the kingdom were stopped, one-by-one, and the bags full of Muck Munchers taken away by several other dolphins under Captain Varkor's control, never to be seen again.

And finally, how Paco and he had been arrested and taken to the dreaded 'hole' in the castle's prison chambers. The most feared of all holding cells known to the world under the sea as the suppression chambers, where most that entered were never heard of or seen again.

Jumper remembered how thankful he was for the important role Sparkles had played in helping them escape from their prison cell.

Sparkles had heard the heartfelt desires from Kevin as he was released from captivity inside Dalina's body each night and left floating on top of the water just above her chamber bed in the water beneath her wonderland bedroom.

Kevin was able to summons Sparkles each and every night and Sparkles was able to reach the large wall of Dalina's sleeping chamber and talk to Kevin as he floated on top of the water.

At high-tide, which was every night while Dalina slept, Sparkles was able to climb up on top of the wall of the chamber and actually see Kevin floating in hundreds of small peaces and as Kevin spoke, the pieces that were his mouth moved together enough to form his words so he could whisper his desires to Sparkles, telling her of Lundon's whereabouts and how Sparkles could actually help Jumper and Paco escape from the prison suppression chamber.

Snapping back to the moment of reality from inside the cave, Jumper and Paco pondered their queen's harsh words directed at them. Her words had cut right through Jumper's and Paco's hearts. They knew that if their queen thought of them as traitors, then the rest of the fish population surely felt the same.

Princess Pompom had perked up when she heard her mother's voice, and acted like she couldn't wait to run out and give her mother a big hug and kiss. King Pom placed one of his tentacles on his daughter's shoulder. He, too, felt like hurrying out to greet his wife, but he knew that they had to time their entrance just right to make sure Varkor could not stop them this time.

"Traitor?" King Pom whispered. "Don't worry Jumper, she'll soon know who the real traitor is," he proclaimed.

"But I wished for her to be a good queen!" Lundon said, confused at why she'd not become good instantly.

"My mother just needs to see me and my father! She has to know we are alive," Pompom said as she dashed out through the opening of the shell cave.

"No!" Waxer yelled. "Princess! Not yet..."

It was too late and now that Princess Pompom had taken the first step, the others knew they must join her, if nothing more than to protect her. They swam out through the entrance to face their enemy.

Seeing King Pom and Princess Pompom, Varkor could not believe his eyes. Hatred filled his heart and he knew each and every one of his lies and deceptions would be exposed, not only to the queen, but to the entire kingdom, as well. Varkor knew that he had only one chance to save himself and that he only had seconds in which to do it.

If he could silence the king and his daughter, before even one word was spoken, then it would be his word against Jumper's and Paco's, and he knew he'd be believed before they would. He could even say they had kidnapped and held the king and his daughter from the beginning. Ready and willing to save his own skin, Varkor positioned himself to fire his most poisonous quills at the young royal who would surely speak first.

Dalina hadn't moved even one inch as she stood there dumbfounded, seeing her daughter and husband. At first she was speechless and the emotions froze her thoughts—her heart. She literally could not move a muscle and was so unprepared for this that she didn't have a clue how to react.

BAM, it hit her and she realized she'd been deceived, and more than that, she realized who had been the real betrayer. That knowledge instantly snapped her back into the reality of what was happening there, and what she was going to have to do.

Fire filled her eyes and revenge pounded her soul. She turned to Varkor and saw that he was seconds away from firing his deadly arsenal of poison quills at her daughter and husband.

"No!" Dalina yelled out, striking Varkor with her tentacle and knocking him off-balance, as his first round of quills shattered on the hard surface of the shell cave wall. "You lied to me!" Dalina screamed as she rushed toward her daughter.

Varkor picked himself up and quickly fired off another batch. The quills, on a direct path toward Princess Pompom, hit Dalina in the back, just seconds before she reached her daughter.

King Pom lunged forward, catching his wife with his outstretched tentacles before she hit the ocean floor.

At that exact moment, Tenoch and Hank Hammerhead moved into position, blocking the path between Varkor and the royals. It was over and Varkor had failed.

Princess Pompom didn't waste one second as she moved to her mother and father's side.

Dalina slowly opened her eyes and looked up at her husband and her daughter.

"Forgive me, my loves," Dalina said, in all humility. "I truly thought that the humans had caused your deaths. I've missed you so, and I didn't know what else to do. I didn't know how else to live without you!"

Dalina then looked directly at Lundon.

"Oh, you precious child, I thought that your belief was my enemy...but it has saved us all! What you have is more powerful than any power I've ever known," she said as she looked up and thought for a short moment, then she turned her head toward her husband. "I have to find the strength to undo all those terrible things I've done, before I...," she couldn't speak the word she was thinking.

King Pom angrily looked up at Varkor and the masses of soldiers that were still facing the royal family.

"Varkor has betrayed all of us!" said King Pom as he held his wife in his tentacles. "Pull from his ranks now or I will consider all of you my enemies as well."

"You are the enemy!" Varkor loudly responded. "This is my kingdom now and it is I, and only I, that they will obey."

"You good soldiers have served this kingdom all your lives," shouted Tenoch. "You know what the Pom family stands for! The choice is yours; make it now! Let's show our king who we are!"

One of Varkor's followers moved over next to Hank Hammerhead, then another, and another and soon there were several at a time making a stand for and with King Pom.

When it was all said and done, Varkor was totally alone; not even one fish-soldier was left on his side. Even the several small snails crawling along the ocean floor tried hard to get some distance between themselves and Varkor. He had started his day in charge of the queen's nation and with one little girl's wish to make a queen good, his power was gone, and the world as he knew it, was lost forever.

The morning sun has begun to appear over the landside of Clearwater and the merry-go-round that Sonia was strapped to was spinning at full speed. The familiar sound of insects humming began to vibrate the rafters of Rolley's carousel building. Sonia opened her eyes and saw that her feet were taking on insect scales with hairy protrusions growing out of her scaly legs. She struggled but could not get off the ride.

Rolley, still at the controls, had almost completely changed into a bizarre human-sized grasshopper. Only his face was recognizable as his former self.

After Sonia saw what he had become, she screamed out, but it sounded more like an insect squealing than a human cry. The more she panicked, the faster her metamorphosis occurred—the faster she turned into an insect.

King Pom was again the head of his kingdom as all of Varkor's soldiers had completely abandoned the new rogue enemy of the fish world.

Varkor slowly started to back up, trying to steal a little distance between him and the masses of his enemies.

"Ancient One!" ordered King Pom. "Apprehend Varkor and escort him to the palace dungeon!"

An ever-so-slight smile graced Tenoch's lips as he immediately lifted his shield and spear and began moving methodically toward Varkor.

In a desperate last effort, Varkor shot his quills at Tenoch, who easily blocked the barrage of needle-sharp bullets with his Aztec shield and kept advancing toward Varkor without losing a beat.

Hank Hammerhead stepped forward, joining Tenoch, letting Varkor know he'd have to take out more than just Tenoch to be free.

Taking Hank Hammerhead's lead, all the other soldiers joined in closing the ranks on Varkor. Varkor continued to move backward as he faced the whole of the royal army. After a short time, though, he realized the only place he'd be able to retreat to was the Decayed Sea.

"You'll all regret this!" Varkor screamed as he continued to move farther back. "I'll return and I WILL take my revenge!"

Moving closer to the black wall, Varkor thought his enemies were only in front of him, but without warning, one gigantic mutant plant popped its ugly head from out of the black, toxic water. At first it did not attack Varkor, instead, it looked around and saw the entire fish army facing off against Varkor. The monster looked at the army, at Varkor, at the army again, and then without another thought, bit into Varkor with its slime-wrenched jagged teeth, pulling him into the Decayed Sea.

The loud, ear-piercing sound of several plant monsters was all that could be heard as they all fought over the one lone meal. After a few moments, the screeching dwindled and only a loud belch from a satisfied mutant plant monster could be heard.

The skeleton of Varkor, picked clean as a whistle, tumbled out from inside the Decayed Sea and floated down to the ocean floor just outside the uninviting wall. The only part of its skinless body that still had any life left in it was the small antenna protruding from its skull. The light at the tip of the antenna slowly blinked on and off, on and off, on and finally—off.

Hank Hammerhead and Tenoch, knowing that the traitor was dead, began to cheer, joined by all the fish-soldiers.

"That was one evil fish," Hank Hammerhead said in his heavy Jamaican accent. "Guess him won't be comin' back after all, mahn."

"Evil always comes back!" commented Tenoch, and with those words, he swam off to continue to provide security to the king and his family. Hank Hammerhead joined Tenoch as he then motioned for his soldiers to leave the royal family to deal with their bittersweet reunion alone.

The masses of fish swam off and were soon out of sight.

Tenoch and Hank Hammerhead stood guard as Jumper, Paco, Lundon, Waxer, King Pom and Princess Pompom were all huddled around Dalina. She lay there wrapped in her husband's tentacles; her eyes closed as he gently placed her down on a large rock. Princess Pompom continued holding onto her mother. Jumper, Lundon, Waxer and Paco moved up to Dalina's side.

Dalina opened her eyes and looked once at her husband, once at Princess Pompom and then up at Lundon. She knew that what she was going to do next would make Lundon one happy little girl. Dalina closed her eyes and Kevin's transparent body started to appear from inside a special pouch located on her waist, one tiny particle at a time. As though they knew they were free, each one had a special bright glow.

The particles swirled around in the water until they were all out of the pouch, and then each particle merged together forming the entire body of Kevin O'Malley. Then, the transparent images ignited like a lit match, and in one big poof, he was in his human form once again, free from Dalina's body—Dalina's spell.

Kevin stood in front of his daughter, still dressed in his scuba gear, with his mask and mouthpiece hanging down from his hip belt. Like Lundon, he was breathing on his own.

"Pops!" Lundon screamed, swimming into his arms.

"You did it!" Kevin said. "You never stopped believing in me, Princess. I love you so much."

Their two bodies, clinging to each other, spun around in circles laughing and crying at the same time.

"But I almost did Pops! It was so hard!" Lundon admitted as she looked up into his eyes.

"I know Baby! I know, but you hung in there," Kevin happily said. "I'm so proud of you!"

Dalina, as though she felt she didn't have much time left, closed her eyes again and soon the water above her head began to churn like a small whirlwind. Princess Pompom and her dad pulled back as the swirl grew larger in a counterclockwise motion and soon it took on the look of a miniature tornado swirling above her head. Though the water above her was in a violent and raging spin, the look on Dalina's face showed contentment and peacefulness.

The merry-go-round at Dalina's wonderland where all the children had been converted suddenly started spinning backwards in the opposite direction. The noise it made acted as a summons to everyone who could hear its message. Miss Hope and Miss Missy rushed into the room and when they saw the carousel spinning in the opposite direction, they knew the nightmare was ending.

"It must be over! She's reversing her spells," said Miss Hope.

"Yes!" screamed Miss Missy. "That means she's letting us go home!"

Cheering and screaming erupted all around the room. Even Wart came running in and was elated to see the miracle in motion.

"Come on, everyone!" Miss Hope screamed, as she jumped up onto the turning carousel."

With that, Miss Missy, Wart and all the workers threw down their tools as they, too, hopped on. It was now very clear that everyone around that wonderland had been serving Dalina under a spell. They were ecstatic to think that it was being lifted—that they could finally have their lives back.

A short time thereafter, insects flew in from the opened ceiling and down into the spinning carousel. Somehow, everyone who had been affected by Dalina was drawn in.

There were so many that it looked like all the bugs in the world were returning to the place of their birth. All of the kid-insects seemed joyous and thankful that they were soon going to be 'debugged,' if you will.

Moments later, children and adults alike came sliding out onto the floor. Their bodies had been totally restored. They were happy and laughing as they greeted each other, hugging and kissing.

When Wart came sliding out from inside the ride, he was dressed in a dashing policeman's uniform. It was obvious that he had been a policeman prior to being put under Dalina's spell. While Wart sat there, still a little stunned at what was happening, something inside his shirt pocket began to move around. Then

Wes jumped out, still as a crab creature, and burst into a full-size man right in front of Wart's eyes.

Moments later, Ida, Wes's wife, was released from inside the broken glass tube and shot out of the still spinning carousel, landing right on top of Wes's head.

Everyone, especially the children stopped cheering and laughing as they stared down at the man and woman who had kidnapped them.

"Wait a minute," Wart said, looking closely at the two. "You're the same as you were. You weren't under any spell! You're just pure bad; both of you, just pure bad!"

Wart grabbed Wes and Ida by the back of their collars and started leading them to the door. Wes looked around at all the kids, trying to spot Waxer.

"Where is dat brat?" Wes yelled as Wart dragged him and his extremely ugly wife away. "I swear I'll kill dat one if'n I ever see him again! I swear on yer grave, crazy lady!"

"Shut up you ol' swamp scum! Just shut up!" Ida shouted back at Wes as they got closer to the door.

"You both have the right to remain silent," Wart said in his deep but very excited voice. "That means you can shut those almost-toothless mouths of yours. Anything you say can be used against you in a court of law. Actually, anything you say can cause me to knock the few teeth you have left right out of your mouths...." With that, they were out the door and gone.

Within seconds of the large doors slamming shut, the remaining folks in that large room exploded into loud cheers and blissful celebration.

Sonia was now more than halfway converted into a grasshopper as the spin of the circular ride had reached its top speed. With only minutes left before she would be entirely converted, a grossly deformed Rolley moved next to her, watching and waiting for his new mate to be completely transformed.

Suddenly, the merry-go-round began to slow down, and then it stopped; and, like the carousel in New Orleans, it started to reverse its direction, moving counterclockwise. At first, Rolley was confused at what was happening, but then it hit him and he realized exactly what was going on. As the thing began to pick up speed, he looked down at his arms and saw that they were changing back to a human form.

"Yes!" Rolley yelled. "Yes! The spell is broken! We're free! Sonia! We're free!"

At the entrance to the carousel building, Wanda Worthington had been trying to get in through the locked door. She looked through the small window and could see what was happening inside. She screamed Sonia's name and continued to hammer on the door trying to get Sonia's attention. By then the carousel was again spinning at warp speed and the two on it were nothing more than two blurred images, scaring Wanda even more.

Soon, however, Sonia's screams turned from the high-pitched shriek to her human voice, and then both Sonia and Rolley came sliding off the spinning carousel, landing a few feet away from each other. Sonia looked at her arms and legs and they had been returned to normal. She looked up at Rolley and he, too, was human.

Rolley smiled and nodded his head. "Go for it, Sonia! You can do it! It's all up to you now!"

Sonia knew exactly what Rolley meant as she stood up and ran out of the building and right past Wanda.

"Come on! I now know what was missing! I know how to get our kids back!" Sonia yelled, not missing a beat.

Not understanding what was actually going on, Wanda followed after Sonia as new hope rushed into her heart, too.

With Queen Dalina and the others watching, Waxer was spinning wildly in a counterclockwise motion. Right in front of their eyes, he turned from a cute, fun-loving dragonfly back into his human form. He soon stopped spinning and fell down, straddling Jumper's head and back.

The water above Dalina's head finally returned to a calm, peaceful motion. Waxer swam off Jumper's head and was happy that he had been turned back into a boy, and, like Lundon and Kevin, was able to be there under the water and still breathe.

"Oh, he's really cute!" Pompom whispered as she leaned over to Lundon's ear allowing only her to hear.

"Ewwww! No way!" was all that Lundon could say, clearly showing the number of years' difference in hers and Princess Pompom's ages.

"It's done...my spells are broken!" Dalina said. "I hope Lundon's dear mother will be able to forgive me."

Princess Pompom moved closer and hugged her mother.

Dalina hugged her precious daughter back, sitting up and showing everyone that she would be okay and that Varkor's poison was no match for a mother's love for her family.

Off to the side, hiding behind some rocks was Sparkles, smiling from ear-to-ear now that things seemed to be getting back to normal. Suddenly, though, she turned her head up toward the land and in an instant, she darted off in that direction.

"Your Good Queen Majesty?" Lundon said moving up to Dalina's side. "What do you mean you hope my mother will be able to forgive you? She's okay, isn't she?"

Smiling, Dalina reached out and gently touched Lundon's hand.

"She's more than fine, child. Listen! She's calling for both of you right now!"

"Lundon! Kevin!" Sonia screamed as she continued running toward the water. "I love you guys and I know you are alive down there! I know it! I BELIEVE!" she screamed, letting the whole world know that she had been wrong about Lundon's and Kevin's friends from under the sea. She was not afraid of the water any longer and ran into the surf without hesitating.

Sparkles floated up right in front of Sonia—and Sonia, ecstatic to see her again, reached down and picked her up.

"Sparkles! I knew you'd come! I believe now!" Sonia said, kissing and caressing the cute little starfish.

Sparkles really enjoyed the hugs and kisses and attention Sonia was sharing with her.

"Watch what can happen now that you believe!" Sparkles said, smiling the cutest smile that Sonia had ever seen in her life.

Wanda and Rolley stopped at the water's edge and watched. Both knew that they were witnessing one of the greatest moments in their lives.

"You believe it sister! YES!" screamed Wanda.

"Yeah! Go for it, Lady! This time it's really yours," Rolley echoed.

Sonia kissed Sparkles again, and like Lundon had done before, placed her cute new friend back into the water. Just as Sparkles' body touched the salty surf, a bright gold color shot out from her tips. Then a glorious rumbling sound erupted, and the whole sky lit up from the reflection of the gold color as it spread over the water covering the whole area, clear out to where Kevin's boat used to anchor.

Out a bit from the beach and down under the water was Lundon's Popsicle-stick bridge, resting on the ocean floor where it had landed the day Lundon had been taken away. It, too, began to shake and rumble and then it started to grow bigger, bigger, and even bigger still, and soon it reached from the ocean floor to the top of the water.

The bridge emerged from out of the ocean, thousands of times larger and still growing. Soon, the unearthly glow collected onto the sticks of the bridge, giving it a shiny, bright gold coating. Finally the bridge reached the sandy beach, with one end staying submerged under the water and the other end resting on the dry sand just a few feet away from where Sonia was standing. It now connected both worlds forever...a passageway for those who would believe—for those who possess the Three Keys.

As Sonia, Wanda and Rolley stood watching this whole spectacular event unfold, Kevin, Lundon and Waxer, like Three Musketeers, walked out of the ocean over the large bridge. As Lundon had professed so many times before, when her father's work was finished under the sea, he would be coming home. She just didn't know when she made those claims, that it would require her whole family being there to help finish the task.

Sonia stepped up onto the bridge and began running to join her family. Lundon met Sonia first and jumped into her mother's arms. Sonia hugged and kissed Lundon like she'd done in every one of her dreams since the day Lundon went missing. Then, she looked back toward the ocean side of the bridge, silhouetted in front of the promising morning sky was Kevin, standing tall and gazing back at Sonia. They walked into each other's arms.

Lundon beamed as she watched the two loves of her life embrace, and then she walked to them and joined the hug-fest. She had waited for this moment for such a long, long time. She knew then what believing in someone really meant. That love, belief, and the impossible, are three things that not only have real meaning; they cause real things to happen.

Watching all this from the waterside of the bridge was Jumper, Paco, Pompom, King Pom and Queen Dalina. They, too, were enjoying the magic that had touched the two worlds, celebrating for the first time the doors in this world the three keys can actually open.

Sparkles moved to the edge of the surf, up next to where Rolley had sat down. They looked at each other and then like it was as normal as could be, Sparkles raised her one arm as Rolley lifted his finger and they both slapped them together in a semi high-five.

"Hey! Wanda!" Waxer said as he walked down the bridge onto the sand, and up to his mother.

"I guess you were right about that bridging stuff and, and a lot of other stuff, too."

Waxer stood there, not having a clue of what he needed to do next. So, after a moment of looking him over, Wanda reached up and pulled him closer to her, hugging him with all the warmth a mother could give to a child.

"I love you, son!" Wanda whispered.

Waxer looked into her eyes. He was going to say something he'd never said to her before.

"I love you too, Mom!"

Waxer and Wanda—mother and son, held each other tight.

No one really knew until that very moment in time what Lundon O'Malley had done with her Popsicle-stick bridge—a bridge built out of love for, and belief in, her family and the power of believing in what most think is impossible.

The End

What if Hollywood gave 50% of one of its hit movies to benefit American schools?

There would be millions of dollars given to our schools!

The toy stores and bookstores wouldn't be too happy, would they?

Well...

This part of Hollywood is giving back!

50% of the profits of this entire franchise—books, movies, and all merchandising sold in the United States, will be given to American schools.

Don't put your hard-earned money into the pockets of the toy stores, bookstores, or department stores. Put it where it will count the most, back into our schools!

An Entertainment Fundraising Campaign

Instead of traveling to your local bookstore or toy store, just go to one of your local schools or go on-line to:

www.lundons.com

Here is a list of merchandise relating to this story you may want to have for yourself:

Backpacks with characters from the story.
Lunchboxes with one or more of your favorite characters.
Character-covered notebooks.
T-shirts with characters.
Character-shaped erasers.
Posters of each character.
Hardback copy of the book.
Posters with multiple characters, and much, much more!

50% of U.S. profits from these items go back to American schools!

An Entertainment Fundraising Campaign!

ABOUT THE CREATORS OF THE STORY

A LITTLE HISTORY

As told by Dennis H. Christen and Craig S. Zukowski

Hi, Dennis here. I'll start the story and Craig will finish it. It all started in 1979, while playing with my 3 year-old daughter, Lundon, at the Santa Monica beach in California, I noticed that Lundon, without any hesitation, took the hand of a stranger who just happened by. I didn't know if the older gentleman had asked for her hand or if she thought it was my hand. Still, she walked with him. By the time I could stand to go and retrieve my baby girl, she'd pulled away and was running back toward me. The man looked at her and smiled, but just kept walking away.

That evening, overwhelmed with what could have happened to her, I began making notes for a story about child stealing; and within a few months I finished a screenplay called "Lundon's Bridges."

It took on several more re-writes over the next few years, and then I had to put it away while I went to South Korea to do a mini-series. After staying in Korea for the next 12 years acting in Korean television and movies, I became touched by the people and the stories of the Korean War, and was compelled to write and later produced a movie called "Soldiers of Innocence." It ended up winning Korea's Grand Bell Award, their equivalent to America's Oscar. Having that under my belt, I felt ready to return to my baby; "Lundon's Bridges," and started playing with it again. By then approximately ten years had come and gone.

By 1991, I was back in the United States and was in development at a major Hollywood studio, working on three of my projects, "Lundon's Bridges" was one of them. While there, I was advised by my development representative that due to the success of a live-action/animated film called, "Who Framed Roger Rabbit," that they would like to see me find an animator and try and re-write or re-develop the story into a live-action/animated format.

That idea excited the dickens out of me, but I had never met an animator before, and didn't have a clue as to how to find one. I left the studio for lunch and ended up sitting next to a man named Craig Zukowski who had just left his studio as a newly, that very morning, unemployed 'animation producer.' Hanna-Barbera had just cancelled the show he was producing called, "A Pup Named Scooby Doo," and Craig had, whether by fate or pure coincidence, entered the same restaurant that I was lunching at. To make it even more bizarre, he picked a seat right next to me at the counter. He claimed later that he'd never sat at a counter to eat his lunch before and really didn't know why he decided to that day.

Hi, I'm Craig and I'll take the story from here. As Dennis mentioned, I sat at the counter between him and another gentlemen. They were in a heavy conversation and as I ate my food, I overheard Dennis talking about Korea. I injected that I had worked in Korea as a supervisor on an animation series. After learning Dennis was an actor there, I realized that he was the American Actor that had his face on this massive marquee I saw with my Korean translator. She asked if, and hoped that, I knew him. Saying he was famous in Korea and she was a big fan. I had to tell her I was just an animator and that we don't get to meet actors all that often. She thought because we both were from Hollywood that surely we not only knew each other, but that we were also friends. I know she was secretly hoping that I could arrange for her to meet him.

Now I found myself not only sitting next to Dennis, but talking about getting involved in "Lundon's Bridges." We met that night for a traditional Korean dinner in Koreatown and spent the next two and a half years developing and writing the screenplay from Dennis' original story. We both literally stopped everything we were doing in our lives to write and develop that story. The end result of that collaboration was "Lundon's Bridge and The Three Keys," the first of a multi-book series in the Lundon's Bridge Franchise.

Dennis was born in Lehi, Utah in 1948. After growing up in California and Utah, he joined the army the day after graduating from high school and subsequently served in Korea from 1966 to 1969. After successfully completing his military service, Dennis spent a two-semester stint at Brigham Young University. However, he could not resist the call of Hollywood and left to pursue his dreams of acting and writing.

During the long, drawn-out actor strike of 1980, Dennis was cast to do a miniseries in South Korea. After finishing the initial series, he was offered additional roles. However, to do so, he was required to learn to read, write and speak the Korean language. Dennis quickly began to learn the language and an original three-month stay turned into almost 12 years. He established a solid career as an actor in Korea becoming a star on one of the most successful daily sitcoms in Korean television history called, "A High Schooler's Diary" (Ko-kyo Sang-il-gee).

During his years in Korea, Dennis performed in over 640 episodic television shows, miniseries, movies of the week and feature films, which took him to 12 different countries. The last and most prestigious miniseries was the award winning 38-hour program called, "The Eyes of Dawn" (Yo-myong-wee Noon-dong-ja). During the 1980's in Korea, foreign actors were not considered for awards. So instead of the normal Korean version of the Emmy, Dennis was given a Special Acting Award for his role in the first all-English language Movie of the Week that had been produced in Korea. The English title was "A Tear for My Enemy" (In-kan-kwa Chun-jang). Dennis was the first foreign actor to be placed on the Korean TV Guide list of the 50 most popular entertainers in Korea. Dennis was also the first non-Korean actor allowed to join the Korea Television Actor's Association. It was during one of the association functions that he met his wife, Korean actress Eun Kyong Seo.

Eventually, Dennis stepped behind the camera as an assistant director for a Cannon Group film called, "Field of Honor." He then wrote, starred in, and produced the award winning feature film "Soldiers of Innocence." The film was nominated for two Grand Bell Awards (Korea's equivalent of the Academy Award) and won for Best New Director.

Dennis authored a non-fiction book, "Rape? Not Me!!" That book, the first for Dennis, was published in 1974. He has subsequently written several screenplays for motion pictures and television.

Dennis is currently based in Beverly Hills, California and is a fulltime actor/writer/producer. In 2002 his novel, "Dennis H. Christen's Madam, The Grass Is High," a romantic comedy love story about the old for the young, was published and is presently being sold worldwide. The newest release now ready for public consumption is Dennis' 1976 start, "Lundon's Bridge and the Three Keys." a story about a heroic young girl who wins a war between the land and the sea using nothing more than her love and belief in her parents. Both novels will be turned into feature films.

Dennis H. Christen
(As an Actor)
-Film-
Title/Role/Country
"One Woman" Jonathan Wayne (Korean)
Korean Title: "Han Yo-jha"

"The Last Train" Corporal Smith (Korean)
Korean Title: "Mageemak Gi-cha"

"Soldiers of Innocence" Sgt. Collins (U.S./Korean)
Nominated for two Golden Bell Awards Korea's equivalent to the Oscar and won one for Best New Director in 1990.

-Television-
Title/Role/Network and Country
"A High Schooler's Diary" Mr. Wilson (KBS-TV Korea)
(460 Episodic Emmy Award winning Sitcom)

"The Tough Time" Minister Webber (KBS-TV Korea)
(52 hour miniseries)

"The Raging Sea" Rudolph (KBS-TV Korea)
(7 hour miniseries)

"A Tear for My Enemy" Lt. Gray (KBS-TV Korea)
Special Acting Award for Dennis

"The Green Mirage" (18 hour miniseries Korean)

"The Eyes of Dawn" (38 hour miniseries Korean)

Craig was born in Cleveland, Ohio in 1952 where he lived until David Cody, a high school art teacher helped him get a one semester scholarships that took him to the Columbus College of Art and Design, where he received another scholarship and a rigid foundation in traditional art and design. Disillusioned with advertising and illustration, he dropped out.

Now, while trying to be a team player working in the family's small metal shop, his mind would travel off into the world of fantasy; where the pounding reverberation of the punch presses became the musical footsteps taking him away from realities of the workday.

Ah! But a dancer brought him back with an austere question:

"What happened to your passion?" She then took him to an Alvin Nicolai Dance Company production. Under the show's seduction, he conjures up abstract kinetics, sweating drama, while feeling the chilling music. The idealistic romantic now knew what was needed to aid and abet his paint brush. He skillfully took this enlightenment, escaping a doomed destiny in the factory to attend the prestigious San Francisco Art Institute, where in 1976 he earned his Bachelor of Fine Arts Degree in cinematography.

With only two years of classic art training and two years of a San Francisco avant-garde approach to filmmaking, something Hollywood shunned, Craig arrived at Hollywood and Vine and began knocking on doors.

As luck would have it a 'gracious' producer actually took the time to enlighten him. Letting him know that there really is no such thing as a filmmaker in Hollywood and that you're either a script writer, a cameraman, or a gaffer, etc. He told Craig to go back to where he came from and not to come back until he had a real job title, one that he was properly trained for.

Slammed into reality, the naive dreamer found his way to Hanna-Barbara, where they surmised that since he was half-artist half-filmmaker, he must be an animator or maybe even a storyboard artist. He began training that day, and within a few weeks he had an actual job with a title.

Though Craig stepped into the magical world of animation as just a temporary job, his career has spanned working all over the world with companies such as: TFC Trikompany, Cinar, Dragon Entertainment, Hyperion, MGM, Animation, D.I.C. Group, Hanna-Barbera Productions, Fil Cartoons, King Features, Marcami-Wolf-Swenson, Marvel Productions, Filmation, and the infamous Ralph Bakshi Production.

Craig took on an executive vice-president's role with Dragon Entertainment of Los Angeles where his duties included marketing, sales, budgeting, and co-production efforts.

Craig joined Dennis Christen in 1991 and started collaboration on Dennis' non-animated script, "Lundon Bridges". After two and a half long years of collaboration with Dennis, "Lundon's Bridge and the Three Keys," the first of 5 books of the "Lundon's Bridge" franchise, was born.

Be on the lookout for Craig's first book of illustrations from his "Lundon's Bridge and the Three Keys," illustration scrapbook. Many of the characters never survived the 'edit' process, but still belong to the list of Lundon's illustrations by Craig S. Zukowski. That book will follow shortly after Book 1 has reached its audience.

A list of his actual production credits reads like a Who's Who in animation:

Craig S. Zukowski
(as an In Betweener)
"Super Friends" (Hanna-Barbera Prods)

(as a Storyboard Artist)
"Defenders of the Earth" (Marvel Productions)
"Muppet Babies" (Marvel Productions)
"The Teenage Mutant Ninja Turtles" Marrcami-Wolf-Swenson)

(as an Assistant Animator)
"Smurfs" (Hanna-Barbera Productions)
"Fat Albert" (Filmation)
"He-Man" (Filmation)
"Lord of the Rings" (Bakshi Productions)

(as an Animator)
"American Pop" (Bakshi Prods—Rotoscope)

(as an Art Director)
"Double Dragons" (13 Episodes) (D.I.C. Group)

"Hurricanes" (13 Episodes)

(as a Director)
"Beverly Hills Teens" (65 episodes) (D.I.C. Group)

(as an Overseas Animation Supervisor)
"Defenders of the Earth" (11 Episodes) (Marvel Prods)
"Blondie & Dagwood" (CBS Primetime Special)
"The Bible Story" (Hanna-Barbera Productions)
"Bill & Ted's Excellent Adventures" (13 Episodes) (D.I.C.)
"Babes in Toyland" (MGM Animation)
"Life with Louie" (26 Episodes) (Hyperion)
"Country Mouse City Mouse" (18 Episodes) (Cinar)
"Arthur" (20-11 min. Episodes) (Cinar)
"Arthur" (1-15 min. video) (Cinar)
"Arthur (54 min. Christmas Special) (Cinar)
"Werner 4" (Feature Film) (TFC Trikompany)

(as an X-Sheet Timer)
"World Reporters" (TV) (TFC Trikompany)
"Dieter" (Feature Film) (TFC)
"Derrick" (Feature Film) (TFC)

LUNDON'S
BRIDGE
WWW.LUNDONS.COM

12640138R00140

Made in the USA
Lexington, KY
20 December 2011